SCOURGE

A SNOWBOOKS HORROR NOVELLA

Proudly published by Snowbooks

Copyright © 2016 Gary Fry

Snowbooks Ltd.
email: info@snowbooks.com
www.snowbooks.com.

British Library Cataloguing in Publication Data.
A catalogue record for this book is available
from the British Library.

Paperback: 978-1-911390-81-7
Ebook: 978-1-911390-82-4

SCOURGE

GARY FRY

SCOURGE

ONE

"All right, mate, how ya doing?" said John Marsh, raising a half-empty pint glass to greet me.

I recognised the man's bullish attitude from about twenty years ago, when he, my brother and I had worked together on building sites. A lot had changed since those days, especially for me, but as John was still in the trade, his colleagues surely wouldn't allow anything other than such a robust manner.

"I'm doing okay," I replied, sitting opposite him at a bar table with the glass of red wine I'd bought after entering the city centre pub. Bradford had changed a lot since our youthful drinking days; I couldn't even remember the last time I'd visited. There were reasons for that, of course — painful memories involving family, especially Glenn, my late brother — but I hadn't come to dwell on that. The truth was that I'd just attended a university meeting about some collaborative research concerning social mobility. And after bumping into John in front of the city hall — Christ, what were the chances? — we'd arranged to meet for a lunchtime drink.

"I'll say you're doing well," said John, reaching across the table to tweak the lapels of my smart jacket. He was dressed in builder's gear and would return to work on a nearby site that afternoon. "What are you now — *professor*, is it?"

"Just a doctor," I replied, feeling a little uncomfortable. The pub was full of blue-collar types, all sinking needful beers and convenient lunches. It wasn't that I thought I didn't fit in anymore; it was more to do with not wanting to come across as "above my station", quite a sin for working-class-types-made-good. "I'm involved in psychology at the moment. It's all very interesting."

Just then, John's face changed, and I didn't need to draw on my knowledge of body language to realise that something troubled him. In fact, I'd sensed this outside earlier, when he'd suggested that we might break bread and catch up. He'd looked tired, haunted, worried. I was convinced that he'd wanted to talk about something more than our shared, distant pasts.

And so it proved. Following another ten minutes of small talk, during which we both delivered info-dump résumés of our activities since earlier life — a marriage, mortgage, kids for him; education, career, bachelordom for me — he lapsed into confessional mode, shuffling his chair my way, the manoeuvre facilitated by the few pints he'd already powered back.

"Doing what you do for a living," he said, his voice now little more than a tremble, "I wonder if you could...well, *help* me."

"Yes, I'll try," I replied, wondering where this was heading. Despite having published widely in the field of social psychology and developed an international reputation from my Oxford academic base, I was far from a household name and certainly no mental wand-waver. "What's the problem, mate?"

The chummy nature of this invitation appeared to hearten him, to such a degree that he immediately went on.

"I've seen something recently — something *unpleasant*." I was certainly intrigued. I said so, and then asked him to continue.

"You promise you'll keep this to yourself? That it'll remain — what's the word — *confidential?*"

"My lips are sealed, pal. And you've no idea just how trustworthy I am in this regard. Ethics committees — bane of my fucking life."

He smiled, an expression that sat awkwardly on his pale, agitated face. But moments later, he launched into a decidedly strange monologue.

He told me that he'd been working lately on a large building project in Bradford, the demolition of an old shopping complex and preparation for a new retail centre, to attract folk back to the dying place. I knew what he meant; the city, once such an important industrial centre, the heart of the world's wool trade, had since become a ghost town, full of empty mills and failing high street stores. Investors, looking to make fast money in hip 'n' happening locations, got no further than Leeds nearby, just off the motorway hotline to London and the rest of the world. Bradford, by contrast, was like a forgotten little brother.

Something about this train of thoughts, the way it related to Glenn, my late sibling (whom my informant had known well), refocused my attention on the guy's words. Surely nothing he told me could be worse than *that* horror, a fatal drug overdose in some local nightclub.

But then John Marsh drove my creeping unease even deeper.

"The other night, on the late shift," he said, having taken another lengthy slurp of beer, "I saw something that…that made me question my mind."

"Your *mind*?"

"Yeah. You know what I mean. All those drugs we used to do. Es. Weed. Acid."

It had been a long time ago — we'd all been young and stupid, especially Glenn, who, it had proved, had been stupidest of all. But I didn't understand what John was getting at. Was he fearful

3

of flashbacks, and asking me, a supposed expert in psychology, to either confirm or deny the experience he'd alluded to? But to do that, I had to know what the "unpleasant" thing he'd seen was. Then he told me.

"I was on my own, staring out across the building site. We'd just spent the day scraping away all the rubble with diggers, ready for foundations to be sunk. That was when...when I saw something lurking at the back of the site. At first, I thought it was just a kid fucking about, the way they do around here, what with few jobs and nothing to do but cause menace. But then I wasn't so sure."

"How do you mean, John?" I asked, deliberately using his Christian name, even though as kids, we'd referred to each other by disrespectful surnames or even worse — anything to maximise mutual discomfort. Such is the emotional maturity of working-class young men.

But now the guy, a fully grown adult, was getting to the gist of his tale. While doing so, he sounded like a frightened child.

"This thing — this *figure* — didn't look human... not entirely, anyway."

"Go on."

"Well, for one thing, it had *yellow eyes*. Fucking *yellow*."

All this, John had claimed, had happened at night-time; the dark did strange things to human vision, moonlight and streetlamps hardly helping. But I said nothing, simply letting my old friend continue.

"And its legs — maybe even its arms..."

"What about them?"

"They... they *didn't bend the right way*. Or rather, they did, but only occasionally. At other times, they went in the *other* direction, as if the knee joints and elbows were... well, double-hinged."

More tricks of the light, perhaps — or maybe an absence of it. During my studies, I'd seen the silhouetted figure of a ballet dancer swirling on the spot; it was possible to perceive this girl turning one way or the other — clockwise or widdershins — depending on which mind-set you adopted. Switching from one perception to the next was trickier than might be imagined. The human mind was an impressive bit of kit, but could be bloody docile at times.

At any rate, as John babbled on about how stupid all this must sound and asked me if I thought he might have experienced one of those well-known "acid flashbacks", I struggled to suppress another concern, one lurking at the core of my brain, even further back in memory than John's and my early days together, along with my long-dead brother who'd been even less fortunate with drugs than John considered himself now.

TWO

While making my excuses and promising my old friend that I'd be in touch (we'd exchanged mobile numbers) once I'd consulted a colleague with experience in the field, I noticed a young man standing on the far side of the bar wearing sunglasses. Now mid-October, it wasn't a bright day, and indoors there was even less to shield the eyes against, so I wondered why he was making such a foolish fashion statement. It couldn't be easy seeing behind those lenses, maybe as hard as it had been for John to see the other night, when he'd spotted his creepy interloper. At any rate, as I watched this potential observer (that's the other thing about shades; onlookers can never tell where the wearer is gazing), John made a final comment before going to the bar for more beer.

"I just couldn't make the thing out. Even though all its limbs pointed one way, unlike usual human bones, the head sometimes faced backwards, with those eyes — bright yellow in the moonlight — looking my way... "

Then I left him to his lunchtime excesses, wondering how many employment rules he'd be breaking after returning to the building site with at least three pints inside him.

But as I fled the pub (refusing to look again at that man wearing sunglasses, now seated in one corner), I recalled that some people could tolerate more toxins in their systems than others, almost certainly a biologically determined capacity. That was surely how Glenn had died, the indulgent, jobless scrotes he'd hung around with at the time, while John and I had been out working, responding to a cocktail of booze and pills with less tragic consequences. But again, I didn't want to think about that; returning to Bradford this week had inevitably brought it all back to my attention, and I should resist it at all costs.

My university meeting had occurred that morning, and now — a Wednesday — I had time free until the weekend, when I planned to attend the region's famous mela festival. Bradford had recently been declared a "city of sanctuary", in celebration of its ethnic diversity and ostensible tolerance of different cultures. This glossy, high profile award concealed some complex social problems, however, and a regular outbreak of race riots and communal frictions arising from various groups living together cheek-by-jowl had given the place a dubious reputation.

I confess that I'd never been a hometown apologist, and had been delighted to leave to study as an undergraduate in London about fifteen years earlier. After my brother's death, something had been triggered inside me, a sense of the potential futility of existence, and from that time onwards, I'd striven to better myself, moving on from building work and then studying hard, getting the qualifications I needed to take my education further as a relatively late university applicant. Success had followed success, and I was now a senior research fellow, specialising in social group behaviour, the interrelations of subpopulations.

It was perhaps odd that I'd never considered Bradford a suitable place to conduct psychological studies. With the exception of a few other cities and some London boroughs, the place had the most diverse population in the UK, with only two-thirds of it White British natives, and the rest mainly a composite of Asian and other Black nationals. The annual mela, which in Sanskrit meant "gathering" or "to meet", was an opportunity for representatives of all groups to come together and share their traditions and cuisine. Doing what I did for a living, attendance at this event was essential. The fact that I loved curry was just a bonus, honest, guv.

But the next few days would also be a chance to reacquaint myself with other aspects of the city. After all, social tensions aside, it had a lot going for it. Dating back centuries — when it had been known as "broad ford", because the town had spanned a significant body of water — it had since developed into a thriving centre of trade and industry, particularly during the nineteenth century, when factory pioneers and business entrepreneurs had placed it firmly on the world map. Its proximity to the Yorkshire Dales and a plentiful supply of wool had been coupled with good resources of soft water, coal and metals, leading to an explosion of creative ventures, including the construction of countless mills, a new arm of the Leeds-Liverpool canal, and some of the first railway networks in the north of England.

Since that time, especially after the global decline in the wool trade, the city had struggled. Migration, once playing a key role in the provision of local employees, had now become a bone of contention between hard right parties and modern liberal movements; indeed, there was a feeling that the next race-motivated riot was just a single, almost certainly misinterpreted, offensive act away. Poverty was high and employment rates low. Nevertheless, the place had some of the highest ranked schools in the country, while its museums and many churches were great attractions.

And now here I was, for the first time as a mature adult ("Mature? Yeah, *right*," I heard my last girlfriend say in my mind), with so much of it to revisit. I smiled as I passed a new feature of the centre, an artificial lake in front of the city's administrative hall. Heading beyond the combined bus and railway stations, I reassessed multiple streets — so much smaller now — which I'd frequented as a child, just me and Glenn blowing all our spending money in a single Saturday afternoon's decadence.

It wasn't all sweet nostalgia, however. As I walked along some of the darker, less frequented streets, I spotted gangs of non-native youths hanging out together at the ends of alleys, a suspicious lack of beer cans or home-rolled cigarettes among them, as I might have expected if these had been white-British dropout youngsters. Indeed, these guys looked as if they were *plotting* something, maybe more of the unrest to which they resorted after paying ethnic penalties in this country, suffering prejudice on the basis of their skin colour and religious affiliations.

It was dismaying that the whole world had still so much growing up to do, accepting any and all people as its own, but with the political climate the way it was right now, with constant friction in the Middle East and agents of terror ostensibly speaking for all

Asian groups, it simply wasn't that way, and frankly, it looked like years before this might change. And so these misguided people just prepared to retaliate to the next slight, because in such a world as theirs, that was all they could do. It was tragic but true: many were simply detonators looking for explosives.

Keeping myself to myself, I soon moved on and after another few hundred yards, I chanced upon a building site. I immediately thought that this must be the one at which John Marsh was working, its fenced-off stretch of rubble occupied by a number of men in hard hats and presently idle diggers. Overlooked by the shadowy cathedral, I could imagine how my former friend might have misperceived some delinquent out to cause trouble here. This was a poorly lit area, away from the bustle of high streets, where streetlamps were sparse and the moon would claim dominion over all.

But I was being fanciful. The simple truth was the poor fella had probably been overworked lately, the demands of heading up a family while earning a living leading him to hallucinate or rather misinterpret some normal aspect of everyday life. That happened a lot. Hell, without even half the stresses he and many others like him suffered, I'd endured a few edgy episodes down the years, mostly relating to —

But my mind didn't complete that thought, because that was when I saw the symbol spray-painted on a piece of board forming part of the fence around the site. This immediately reminded me of what John's words in the pub had hinted at, some half-buried memory at the core of my mind. A childhood tale, maybe — some urban legend I'd heard as a lad, while occupying this city's streets, with their proximity to so much glorious countryside.

This was what I saw on the board:

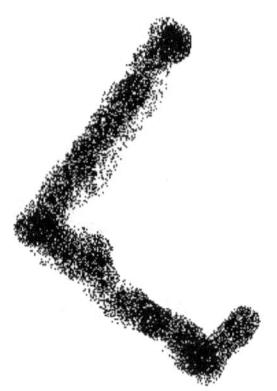

THREE

I'd booked to stay three nights in a hotel just outside the city centre, but within walking distance of its attractions and conveniences. This was quite unlike my rented pad out in the sticks near Oxford, where a lot of my job was carried out, conducting fieldwork in its environs or participating in conference telephone calls from the comfort of my home (and often my bed).

Yes, in terms of my current residential geography (having escaped the grim north), I was lucky, but I'd certainly worked for it and sacrificed plenty. I could never decide whether a wife and kids would have compromised my career or whether the alternative was true, but that was okay. At only thirty-eight, I was happy enough with life and knew there was time yet to follow other pathways if desired.

Back in my top-floor room, I immediately switched on the kettle, had a quick wash, and then booted up my laptop.

Despite being on Annual Leave for the rest of the week, I was sufficiently dedicated to (and obsessed by) my job to check for email regularly. Here was the usual clutch of departmental circulars, along with a few communications from students I'd agreed to supervise. It was a fun way to earn a decent living, and although I could have done much more with my PhD — taken some market-leading post in the private sector, pulling in a six-figure sum each year — I'd always prioritised occupational satisfaction.

But then I spotted a message from someone I didn't recognise.

The university spam-filter was generally effective, binning unwanted communications from benevolent friends in the likes of Nigeria while letting through equally unwelcome (if sadly necessary) requests from my School's Head of Department. Essentially, like some right-wing censorship unit, it eliminated all but selected outsiders, while privileging internal messages. And yet here was contact from an unknown foreigner, some nefarious interloper.

"s.edgely@telegraphandargus.com" read the sender's email address, while its subject title was: "Interview enquiry". I promptly unfurled the full communication and read it at once.

Dear Dr. Parker,

Allow me to introduce myself. I am a journalist with the Telegraph and Argus, which, as you'll know as a native Bradfordian, is the city's newspaper. I learned from contacts at the University that you're in town and wondered whether you'd consent to a short face-to-face interview for a feature we run each Thursday about home-grown people and the work / activities they are involved with. I realise this

is short notice but I'm available today (Wednesday) if convenient for
you? Please let me know at your earliest convenience.

Best wishes —
Sara Edgeley

Making contact the day before the feature's potential publication certainly *was* short notice, but I knew how the world worked, all the polished output from official bodies commonly thrown together in a frenzy just hours before deadline. Or maybe the journalist planned the article to go in the following week's Thursday edition. Either way, I was flattered to have been asked and shot back an immediate reply.

Dear Sara,

Many thanks for your email. I'm not sure why you think I'd be
interesting enough for your readers, but what the hell — let's do this!
If you'd prefer a face-to-face interview, I'm at the Parkhouse Hotel
in Canal Road and can be in the bar at about 4pm today. Would
that give you enough time to produce your article? If so, feel free to
join me.

Regards,
Lee Parker

I'd always found that a little self-deprecation eased any foolish tensions others sometimes developed on the basis of my doctorate. I always flinched when people addressed me in such a formal way. I was "just a fella", as they say — a fella who did reasonably useful work in a relatively important field. But it was no big deal. I wasn't a surgeon who saved lives or a human rights lawyer who did the same. I was just... well, *me*.

When no reply came back inside five minutes, I switched my screen pages to the Internet, my mind returning to the issue raised by chatting with John Marsh and then by what I'd spotted later, on that building site: the symbol spray-painted to a wooden board, which was something I'd *definitely* seen before. Indeed, now I'd had some time to percolate all this material, I realised that something else had risen unbidden to the surface of my psyche.

"Yellow eyes", I thought, typing these words into my favoured search engine. And then I added, "limbs bent in wrong direction", and finally, "head turning over shoulders". I didn't expect much success from such a collection of vague phrases, and so it proved. Amid a number of medical sites devoted to strange conditions rendering human joints overly pliable, I chanced upon a few zoological papers dedicated to creatures with similarly dextrous bodies — cats and insects, mainly. But none of this was what I sought.

Maybe I'd have better luck with a different strategy, one more in keeping with my ill-defined hunch. As a kid, Glenn and I had regularly travelled with our parents (both now deceased, each from cancer in their mid-sixties) to the Yorkshire Dales, where charming tiny villages sat among majestic hillsides and babbling brooks. Those had been wonderful days, the sun shining, pub lunches, games of cricket in sprawling fields. Lord alone knows why our lives had been shattered later, when my brother had overdosed in a Bradford nightclub before he was eighteen years old. But so it goes. Maybe the idyllic nature of our childhoods had been the problem, our loving mum and slightly naïve shopkeeper dad failing to prepare us for all the trials of adulthood. Who knew? Yes, I was a psychologist, but even now, twenty years on from those events, I felt too close to them, as if they were all too emotive...

But I was supposed to be conducting some impromptu research.

Readdressing the laptop, I hacked the following phrase into the search box: "rural / urban myths, Bradford, Yorkshire Dales". Then I hit Find.

I was about to consult the page of instant results when I heard my inbox ping, announcing the arrival of an email. I quickly — perhaps even eagerly, fearful of what I might be about to discover on the Net — flipped back to that page and found a new message from s.edgely@telegraphandargus.com, the journalist who wanted, temporarily at least, to make me feel like a rock star. Chuckling, I opened the email and read:

Lee,
Great — see you there!
S

Well, S's previous deference had certainly crumbled quickly! On this occasion, she hadn't even written "dear", let alone "doctor"! But I wasn't bothered really, in fact preferred my relationships to remain chummy and informal. All that social class stuff folk in the UK worry about was built on tenuous foundations; I should know — I'd spent much of my professional career studying such issues.

But now I had a new matter to preoccupy me. Shutting down Sara's email, I reluctantly readdressed that latest page of search results.

As I suspected, my keywords — "rural / urban myths, Bradford,

Yorkshire Dales" — had generated a lot of tourist-targeted material, mainly advertisements for holiday cottages and splendid walks in the region. But once all the commercial links privileged by mysterious Internet alchemy had died away, I found, from page two onwards, the kind of thing I'd hope to locate.

Here were many pages, most amateur in appearance and as tacky as hell, documenting age-old legends and haunted property right across the county. I'd chanced upon many of these in the past, including headless horsemen; woodland creatures half-man, half-beast; the spirits of wicked landowners tormenting present occupants of great homes; and much more. Every district in the country, possibly even across the planet, had similar stories, a collectively convergent attempt to make sense of the world's complex events, the way the human brain struggled to assimilate everything experience could throw at it.

So much for that, I thought, but then I spotted what I'd half-hoped, half-feared to discover.

The myth of the *felachnids*.

There wasn't much material here, just a poorly written paragraph mentioning what John Marsh had referred to: the yellow eyes, the double-jointed limbs, the heads that turned backwards whenever that was necessary. These creatures, which otherwise resembled humans, appeared to occupy — or rather, to have once occupied — a small village in North Yorkshire called Nathen, about sixty miles from Bradford, up through the valleys at the foot of which the city rested.

At any rate, I now knew what I'd be doing on my day off tomorrow: travelling north by train and bus.

Because the clincher was the sign by which these ancient entities had been known, something they'd often carved into trees or daubed on stone walls to communicate their menacing presence: a single line like a leg bent at a right-angle across the knee-joint, with a foot tucked inwards, quite the wrong way for any normal person's limb.

FOUR

The journalist arrived bang on time, and by God, if she wasn't good-looking. I'd remained single through choice, preferring the uninhibited lifestyle of an itinerant academic, but I'd had girlfriends from time to time, even though none had stuck around, mainly because they'd wanted the normal things in life, like a mortgage, kids and the rest. I don't know why all this had never appealed to me. A trite psychological explanation might involve Glenn's death and how fundamentally tenuous I believed life was, but frankly, I thought that was bullshit. What might be closer to the truth was the thing had driven me to education and my brother to drugs: our common working-class upbringing had, with its rough schools and teenage tribes, left us deeply mistrustful of others, holding reality at a safe distance, either by abstract theory or hard substances.

Then again, whenever I met anyone like Sara Edgeley, I'd always (temporarily, at least) opened up like a flower-head, drawing in all of the world's beauty.

And a beauty she was. After shaking hands and asking her to join me at a small table bookended by leather couches, I went to the bar to buy the drink she'd requested — a large red wine, same as mine. While waiting for the smart barman to pour the glass and add the cost to my hotel bill, I kept snatching glances back at my visitor and wondered what fickle deities I'd pleased this week. She was frankly stunning, wearing a red dress that rode above her knees and stopped at her shoulders, revealing shapely legs and narrow arms. She was blonde, fair-skinned, and as delicate as some fine porcelain artefact. Her eyes were very definitely blue.

When I turned back to grab the wine, the barman and I exchanged a disturbingly complicit gaze, the kind inscribed in men's DNA, and then I paced back for the table, to sit opposite the woman now slumped on that casual couch. By this time, I wanted to look like George Clooney, but, with my mouth so dry that I had to drink more of my wine, I felt a bit like Elmer Fudd.

Sara had produced a laptop, while I'd left mine upstairs, all its suggestive material about ancient creatures with anatomically impossible limbs driven clean out of mind. I wasn't interested in yellow eyes anymore, but in blue ones — in *hers*. After I asked intuitively if she'd had a long day, she replied, "Every day is long in my game," and then gulped at the large glass of red with needful haste.

Seeing young women neck pints, drain bottles and lay waste to large glasses was hardly a rare sight these days; the impact of feminism and the world of wider work had made such excess inevitable. This amused me, making me realise how elastic human identity was, and how economic necessity — simply earning enough to pay for water, food and shelter — was always its boss.

"I can't say the same pressures are involved in my work," I replied, almost apologetically. After all, why did she want to interview *me*? As a journalist, exposing daily crimes and the malpractice of authorities, *she* was probably a worthier subject for a media feature. But I went along with it all anyway. "I'm actually one of those weird people who *like* their jobs."

That got us going, Sara asking me a number of questions about my past in Bradford and how I believed it related to my career pathway. Mindful of the article's destination — the entertainment section of a local rag — I kept my explanation jargon-free and light-hearted, airbrushing some of its more challenging aspects: leaving school with few qualifications, working briefly in the building trade, returning to education later to reach university. Then Sara asked about my present work, the many publications which had gained some attention on the international scene, and even, in one recent case, at Parliament. I talked — again, quite basically — about my interest in social movements, how different communities integrated...or not, as the case could often be. This was, of course, relevant to my current location — all the ethnic and economic tensions the city had experienced down the years — and readers of its fine newspaper.

I didn't mention my brother, not even once.

It was probably for this reason that I violated the promise I'd made earlier that day. When Sara asked me why I'd returned to my native environment this week, I briefly discussed the meeting I'd had at the university, but also mentioned my newfound desire to reconnect with Bradford, where I'd grown up and where many of my most treasured memories were stored. But then, possibly because the wine had uninhibited me and I hadn't wanted Sara catching scent of Glenn's death, I added something much more indiscrete.

"You know, my work never ends."

"How do you mean, Lee?"

Her eyes were so blue and her legs so long that I had to glance away as I added, "Well, let's just say that today I took on an unexpected research project, one concerning this area's distant past."

"Maybe our readers would be interested in that. Could you say more?"

I could, but I shouldn't...and yet I *did*. What can I say? I just wasn't thinking. I guess I was still trying to keep potential enquiries about any family members still living in the city (there were none) at a distance. Indeed, a few minutes later, I'd told Sara Edgeley, a young journalist who'd surely had some respect for me and my achievements before arriving at the hotel, about a crackpot belief in some local legend, some silly myth concerning yellow-eyed creatures whose limbs and head bent in entirely the wrong directions.

Except that I *didn't* believe in this, did I? And so what was its present appeal to me? That question I was unable to answer. Maybe it had some subconscious connection to my late brother; after all, my informant — the surely deluded man who actually thought he'd seen one of these unlikely things — had been one of Glenn's and my friends from our youths, a drinking companion, a guy with whom we'd once taken so many shitty drugs. Hell, it was all very complicated. But in light of what happened the next day, the stream of creepy events triggered off, I'm just glad I didn't mention John Marsh by name.

However, right then, now the interview appeared to be over, I was more concerned with what might happen that evening.

"Can I get you another drink?" I asked, noticing that, while I'd babbled on, Sara had finished her wine.

She gave me a look as if to say: *But my task is complete and I have to return to the office, write up the interview, and get it to the page designer immediately.* But we live in a very different world these days, one in which as much work can be done remotely as at places of employment. Indeed, after saying she'd need about half an hour's silence to turn her notes into the short article, she agreed to the drink and then started typing.

Once she was done, she glanced up and said, "We usually arrange for a photographer to visit, but as this is so short notice, I fished a stock image of you from Oxford's website. We can use that in the article, if that's okay."

"Sure thing," I replied, having consumed only the first third of the fresh glass of wine I'd brought back to the table, before catching up with some e-correspondence on my iphone and eating a sandwich I'd also ordered from the bar (Sara had said she wasn't hungry). Then I said, "But let me ask you one thing."

Sara clicked some laptop keys with a final flourish, presumably attaching the downloaded picture to her text file before firing off the article to go irrevocably into production. "Feel free. The job's done now."

As she closed her computer's lid and settled back to finish off her nearly depleted glass of red (I imagined the pressure of hitting her deadline had made her drink more quickly), I asked, "Why were you so eager to get me in the paper *this* week?"

She smiled, looking innocent, those blue eyes shining in the artificially warm light of the hotel's lounge. There was a window nearby and I could see that it had grown dark outside, all the early evening noises and activities of Bradford — folk fleeing city centre offices, cars and buses stacking up in the rush-hour — muffled by our relatively affluent comfort.

Then Sara said, "Well, I knew you were in town only for a few days, so I thought it would be nice for you to see the feature in print before leaving."

I sensed she wasn't telling me something, and so pushed her a little. "But why are my spider-senses now twitching, suggesting a...well, a less honourable motivation?"

"Bloody psychologists!" she replied, but then laughed, her dextrous legs crossing, leaving more of that red dress to ride up her stocking-free thighs. As I felt something stir inside me, and not in a place I could easily control, she added, "Okay, cards on table. The truth is that somebody let me down at the last minute and I needed a suitable substitute. But that's not to say I don't greatly admire your work."

Now *I* was laughing. "Read much of it, have you?"

"Almost all the book descriptions on *Amazon*, yes."

"That's more than most of my students manage."

"If they're anything like I was as a youngster," Sara went on, draining the last of her drink while I still had a quarter left of mine, "I suspect they're more interested in *other* things."

I both liked and disliked the way she'd made this latest comment, her lips rouged from the last of her wine. Blimey, modern girls could drink, I thought, feeling lightheaded, and then events took a furtive twist. It was obvious there'd been some attraction between us from the moment we'd met — her sassy wit and beauty, my education and status (an Oxford academic, no less) — and it was hardly surprising that, after a brief visit to the hotel's reception to get my single-occupancy double room upgraded (for a few extra quid I certainly wouldn't claim back on expenses), we ended up in bed together, Sara consuming even more alcohol, and me wondering how I'd travel tomorrow with the kind of headache I hadn't suffered since my foolish youth with Glenn, my long-dead younger brother.

FIVE

To say Sara Edgeley was athletic would be a gross understatement, rather like saying cats are sly or dogs subservient. She'd certainly reminded me of my incipient middle-age. Once the light had gone out, she'd removed my clothing as quickly as I'd removed hers, and then she seemed to be everywhere almost at once. Her teeth in particular had been unexpectedly sharp; this was not a feature I'd closely observed before we got down to our business on the bed. But now that the room was pitch-dark, her visually striking attributes had been left to my touch alone, and her modest bites had bordered on causing pain while also heightening the pleasure elicited by her other actions. She'd been a vixen, and despite several moments of astonished unease, I'd enjoyed every part of our frantic lovemaking.

The morning after, I awoke and found her gone, but not in any clichéd Hollywood movie way, the magnificent fuck that's never relocated. In fact, she was in the en suite bathroom with the door locked. When I tried the handle a second time, wondering how, after all we'd done last night, she could feel shy about her body, I heard her call, "I'll be out in a minute, Lee. I'm just putting in my contact lenses."

If that was a euphemism for washing off the smell of sex and sweat, I wasn't about to challenge her. After all, she'd presumably have to visit her office next, while I had the day free to do with as I pleased.

It was now, as I dressed and awaited access to the bathroom, that my mind turned again to my proposed journey, sixty miles north to the village of Nathen, to further my impromptu investigations. It would be nice to explore the region again, having done so regularly as a child. And if, as expected, nothing came of my enquiries with residents up there, I could at least get back to John Marsh and put his mind at rest, maybe with a few psychobabble sound-bites from my much-maligned (rightly so, at times) discipline.

When Sara finally emerged from the bathroom, she was ready to leave and appeared to be in a hurry. She'd have a meeting to attend, probably; it was now near nine o'clock. We kissed and promised to be in touch (yeah, *that* old chestnut) before parting on amicable terms. We'd had a great time together and nobody had been hurt; where was the harm in that?

An hour later, following a mighty breakfast that never seemed to touch my ravenous appetite, I made my way to Bradford's railway station and caught a ride headed ultimately for Newcastle via Leeds, with a stop at Richmond along the way. From that small northern town, I'd take a bus west, delivering me right into the heart of the Yorkshire Dales, where the tiny village of Nathen could be found, the alleged home of the fearsome felachnids.

As varying landscapes slid by — first the industrial scars of Bradford's suburbs and then the swanky finance district of its big city brother and finally the effortless greenery of England's panoramic north — I wondered what devil had got into my head, why I'd chosen to waste a whole day chasing silly age-old inventions. I'd always been of the opinion (as I think are most sensible people) that myths and legends from days of yore were simply primitive attempts to make sense of experiences poorly understood by reason at the time. Their endurance could be ascribed to both their poetic appeal and, less nobly perhaps, to many modern people's reluctance to accept a complex materialistic universe. Why try and understand quantum mechanics when a little green monster with wings and too many eyes can provide a much better story?

But was *I* now entertaining something equally foolish? Had I taken my old friend's story of yellow-eyed, elastic-limbed entities travelling miles from their alleged natural habitat as anything other than an unfortunate neurological event, a perceptual distortion induced by too little light and too much familial or occupational stress?

I'd surely discover more after reaching the village. When this finally happened, following an interminable ride in a bus almost certainly designed without suspension by some disillusioned sadist, I alighted in a charming hamlet, which consisted of nothing more than a crossroads bearing a few shops, a pub and some kind of community hall. Beyond many trees clustered alongside a narrow stream with a stone bridge running over it, a number of residential properties could be seen, each squat and observably reticent. This was hardly a place that loudly broadcasted its existence, and I genuinely believed that if residents could have it erased from all national maps (let alone the ubiquitous Internet), they might have seriously arranged to do so.

I began my research in one of the small stores first, because I was thirsty from the journey and, as this was leisure-time and my university expenses account was suspended, I'd refuse to pay an exorbitant rail price for a cup of tea (once a Yorkshire-man, always one). The shopkeeper was an aged woman with the kind of thinning white hair I could recall my maternal grandmother sporting, before she'd died when I was six or seven. After grabbing a can of coke from a fridge in one corner, I took it to the till-point and then browsed a tall rack of publications, including paperback bestsellers and a number of local history titles. The latter, I thought, might give me a starting point for my enquiries.

"Hello there," I said, smiling my finest smile and relaxing my stilted accent, no longer aspiring to middle Englander status. "I wonder if you can help me on a particular matter."

"I'd be happy to try," replied the amiable woman, whose eyes, I now noticed, were rheumy and bloodshot — certainly far from yellow.

Then I let her know what I was looking for. I approached this potentially thorny issue by suggesting that I was carrying out research for a book of folklore and was keen to gather information about some of the rarer myths and legends from all parts of the country. I told her that I'd read about the felachnids on the Internet and had decided to make the trip north to see what I could discover, since all the World Wide Web had taught me was that the creatures bore peculiar embodied traits and a symbol by which they commonly identified themselves.

By the time I'd finished, the woman looked rather blank, which made me stop to ponder. She was either a fine actress or genuinely knew nothing about the entities to which I'd just alluded.

Nevertheless, after I'd paid for my drink, she suggested I might have "more joy" at the village pub, where, true to every cliché horror films have ever resorted to, I'd almost certainly find an older gentleman, with an interest in local history, who might be able to tell me more.

I thanked the nice old lady and then stepped outside, thinking that if she, clearly a village resident and probably a long-term one, had never heard of the felachnids, the creatures couldn't be *that* notorious, let alone actually exist.

Shaking my head while feeding my coke into one pocket for the journey home — or rather, back to my Bradford-based hotel — I entered the pub at the end of the street and then sought out a guy the shopkeeper had called "Arnold".

The landlord, a burly fellow with a fine moustache, pointed me in the right direction. After giving me change from a fiver for the pint of bitter I'd ordered (no more punchy wine, please, not after last night's excesses), he indicated a man seated alone in one corner, reading a book laid flat on the table in front of him. I quickly crossed the room and then, with a feeble clearing of my throat, drew his attention. He glanced up, little alarm or even intrigue showing in his greenish eyes. It seemed as if he was used to unanticipated company and indeed welcomed it.

A few minutes later, once I'd introduced myself (with honesty on this occasion, imagining the clearly studious guy might respond positively to an Oxbridge scholar) and had been invited to sit alongside him, we fell into animated conversation.

"I do indeed know something about this subject," Arnold said once I'd told him what little I'd already learned. Greatly interested, he'd closed the book he'd been reading earlier, which appeared to be some kind of geological guide, all bird's eye views and cross-sectional illustrations. "As you obviously know, having journeyed here today, the creatures are associated with this village — with Nathen."

I was now excited, mainly because my trip had proved to be worthwhile and I was about to learn something new about the things that had apparently made contact with one of Glenn's and my oldest friends. What with visiting Bradford and bumping into John Marsh, I felt as if I'd plunged back into my youth, and that, in some nebulous fashion, unfinished business was about to be addressed, a way perhaps of coming to terms with what had happened one night in a nightclub twenty years earlier, when I simply hadn't been around to save my younger brother.

Moments later, I listened keenly to what my latest informant had to say.

"The felachnids," — he'd pronounced the first part of their name with a long "eeee" sound, so that the allusion to spiders clearly suggested by "achnids" was tempered by a partial reference to felines, to cats — "are supposed to have come to earth about a thousand years ago, arriving on some rock from another planet. You're right in saying they have...sorry, I mean, *had* yellow eyes and strangely jointed limbs, as well as necks capable of turning right the way round, to look behind them. For this reason, their name — alluding to life-forms quite different from humans, despite their fundamentally similar shape — is rather appropriate, isn't it?"

I could only nod, my own conclusions a moment ago now endorsed by this independent researcher. And, nonsense though it must be, his story of entities arriving from deep space made at least scientific sense, because what species other than something evolving on a different planet could possess such anatomically impossible bodies? Limbs and heads that bent or twisted the wrong way were the stuff of weird gene-pools indeed!

Without interrupting, I attended to what else the man might have to tell me.

"Hey, look," he said eventually, smiling a crooked smile, "I'm no apologist for this kind of thing, and certainly no defender of my ancestors' vivid imaginations. In fact, I'm as sceptical as you now appear."

The truth was that I was captivated, but wasn't about to

disabuse Arnold of his safer interpretation of my facial expression. Then he went on.

"I strongly suspect the felachnids were invented by people once living in Nathen — which is home to about a thousand people and always has been — to account for certain events which occur in all communities, but which, in closely packed and relatively isolated ones like this, can result in particular tensions.

"Imagine one day a loaf of bread goes missing, stolen perhaps by a neighbour. Well, the problem is that you have to live alongside this person for a long time yet, and so it's surely preferable to believe that some *outsider* committed the deed, some impish intruder perhaps emerging from the woodland bordering the village.

"I personally believe that's how the myth arose. The things' dextrous limbs were based on the fact that nobody ever saw these alleged thieves, implying they could make quick getaways, up chimneys or straight out of windows, like the cat-spiders their name suggests. The invaders would also need extremely good vision, being able to look in all directions to watch for observers — hence the back-facing heads. And maybe their yellow eyes, capable of seeing in any kind of light, came from resident sightings overnight of foxes and wolves patrolling Nathen's boundaries.

"Do you see now how the felachnid legend may have arisen? Indeed, according to sources I read many years ago, it wasn't long before these creatures began to be known as the cause of a more insidious violation of the community. I've reviewed a wide range of Middle Ages documents, composed hundreds of years after the myth first appeared in local written materials, and some mention a certain *destabilising influence* at work in Nathen, as if the things had grown more ambitious with time.

"Basically, acts of theft had now been coupled with tricks played on village members. These included property moved from one place to another, suggesting neighbours had in fact taken it. There are other stories about strange cocktails — probably mushroom-based, harvested from the woodland nearby — being administered to people without their awareness; at least that's what anyone caught *tripping* had claimed.

"I think the idea is that, owing to their less than human appearance — those yellow eyes, especially — the creatures were unable to join in the community, getting jobs, mating with people, et cetera. And so they'd elected to lampoon it, to leech off it, to render it edgy and fragile. This was enhanced by the notion that the felachnids were apparently immune to the poison they spread — I mean, they were incapable of intoxication, consuming illicit substances with seemingly no effect at all.

"From our modern, rationalist perspective, these events may have all-too-terrestrial explanations, but again, there's a suggestion that such — what's the word you psychologists use? — that such *projection* served a communal function, removing blame from possibly covetous and indulgent fellow villagers in favour of a belief in some invasive, feckless force trying to steal resources without suffering all the problems actual members of Nathen experienced."

"What you're maybe talking about," I said, finally finding my voice following a period of attentive silence, "is some kind of hardening of paranoiac ways of mass thinking, the kind exhibited...well, by nationalist societies, which tend to achieve union by ascribing all their inevitable imperfections — after all, what social gathering doesn't have such weaknesses? — to an out-group."

"It's interesting to hear you say that," Arnold replied, a wise look on his ageing face, as if he'd already arrived at a similar conclusion, only without a long, expensive education like my own, "because from this period onwards, Nathen became a rather difficult place to engage with, its residents unwelcoming to visitors and even proactively hostile to other villages in the area. There's evidence of at least one mass brawl with the occupants of another residential location nearby, but I'm quite unaware of the reason for this.

"At any rate, all this definitely coincides with more references in written documentation to these *agent provocateurs*, these surely invented entities from beyond the stars, with their impossibly pliable bodies and keenly sharp gazes."

Just then, my informant chuckled, possibly acknowledging the foolishness of his words. After glancing around, I noticed that the pub remained empty this Thursday afternoon, and that even the landlord had vanished from behind the bar. Maybe he'd heard this sort of talk on many a befuddled night; Arnold certainly hadn't been shy in providing his information, as if the knowledge he'd imparted was far from a shameful local secret. Indeed, the aged shopkeeper's ignorance of the myth reassured me that the legend was long-dead, a curio, and even — to those few aware of it — a source of mild amusement.

Nevertheless, something about the stories I'd heard had truly engaged me, capturing my imagination in a way I was unable to assimilate right then. And after draining the last of my pint, from which I'd taken copious gulps while listening to the amateur historian, I made one final point.

"I don't know whether I visited this village as a child," — in my mind, I experienced a flashback of my brother's face, about eight years old, laughing with an innocence which would one day be inexorably shattered — "but I seem to recall a symbol related to the felachnids, a kind of bent limb with an additional part tucked inwards, like a foot at the end of a leg pointed the wrong way."

At that moment, Arnold pushed one hand into his inside jacket pocket and removed a pencil. Then he folded back the cover of the book he'd been reading — that entirely safe text about something tangible, the quantifiable parameters of the humdrum world — and started drawing the image I'd just described. Seconds later, I saw this inscribed on the faded paper:

"That's *it*," I said, eyes surely blazing.

"Yes, that's their sign," my informant replied, his face awash with pride. "Ah, sorry, I mean, that *was* their sign. But the felachnids don't exist, of course. They never did."

SIX

On the bus and then train journey back to Bradford, I was able to process all I'd learned in Nathen, the apparent origin of a group of otherworldly entities who, if my old friend John Marsh's recent eyewitness testimony was true, seemed to have migrated to my native city. Indeed, Arnold had claimed that centuries ago, the creatures had grown more ambitious, trying out new tricks in the village, attempting to destabilise it. And had they now taken an even greater step?

It was the appearance of that symbol — the bent limb boasting an appendage angled impossibly inwards — that refused to let me dismiss the man's account at a glib reductionist stroke. This sign had appeared at the site of the viewing, where that yellow-eyed thing, its arms, legs and head reportedly turned the wrong way, had shuffled around by moonlight, as if up to no good at all.

Vandalism? Was that what this scrote had been attempting to commit? If I, a child of this city, had once been aware of this regional myth, it was possible others would be, too. Some kid, excluded from mainstream society, might have found the felachnid legend imaginatively appealing, adopting their symbol as a mark of affiliation, while continuing to uphold the creatures' nefarious, anti-social habits. Perhaps he'd stolen from shops, too, or maybe even spiked people's drinks in pubs and clubs.

I didn't want to think too hard about this final possibility — after all, I'd once seriously entertained a suspicion that Glenn might have suffered similar, perhaps trying to deny that he'd needed so many drugs — and after disembarking at Bradford's railway station, I reflected again, probably to reassure my flustered self, that the felachnids were just a poetic invention, a way of making sense of a tight-knit community's very ordinary failings. The yellow eyes had been included to encourage villagers to believe that, whatever threat the creatures presented, they could be easily spotted, which would enhance vigilance. And as Arnold had speculated up in Nathen, those twisty-turning limbs, with all their potential for rapid mobility, neatly explained the entities' elusiveness, the reason they'd rarely been observed (except at night in the darkest parts of woodland). In short, the things hadn't been seen directly because — as my informant had also claimed, with eminently sensible reason — they *didn't exist.*

The fact that something didn't ring true about my conclusion troubled me all the way back to my hotel. I'm highly educated, committed to logic, and although tiredness and a residual hang-over from the wine I'd sunk last night with the delectable Sara Edgeley had temporarily blunted my mental abilities, I nonetheless sensed something amiss in this case, as if a component was askew, a strand hanging loose which threatened to tear apart its whole fabric. I'd had similar experiences before, on a number of research projects, and knew that only a good night's sleep and a little unforced reflection could deal with that.

But, now getting on for the late afternoon, life was — as was its impish wont — destined not to be so accommodating.

I guess it was my own fault for checking my iphone. This had become a habit of mine even when off-duty; I could take a month away from work and still suffer a daily impulse to inspect my email. I'd tried telling myself that this was simply a process of spam-deletion, keeping on top of crap everyone is sent online, to avoid tackling it all in one go after my return. But I knew the truth was worse than that. I was basically addicted to my job, and although in many cases that's a positive thing, it often made it difficult for me to switch off. Maybe that was why I was still single.

Anyway, while heading out of the city centre, I browsed my inbox on the tiny screen, wondering which other academics wanted free information now, whether any of my students needed an extension on his or her essay deadline, how many enterprising foreigners were prepared to offer me a cut of their ancestral fortune. But amid a few predictable departmental circulars, there was only one communication that caught my attention, mainly because its subject title read "your interview in the T&A". Having forgotten that this article would appear today, let alone picked up a copy of the local newspaper, I immediately unfurled the email.

Dear Dr. Parker,

I do hope you won't mind me contacting you like this. I found your contact details online after reading the feature about you in today's Telegraph and Argus. I was <u>most</u> intrigued by your latest research interest and may have evidence in support of it. I'd rather not go into details here, but if you could call me on the number included below, I'd be really grateful. Please understand that I am neither a crank nor a timewaster. I'm just very scared and hope you may be able to help. In doing so, I hope I can help you, too.

Best wishes —
Peter Richards

My "latest research project" — did the man mean my work in collaboration with Bradford University, which I'd definitely mentioned to Sara Edgeley yesterday? That was possible, I guessed, but I failed to see how a project concerning social mobility in diverse communities might make someone "very scared", let alone why he'd wish to keep information about that private. In truth, this development puzzled me and even made me feel fearful.

As indicated in his message, Peter Richards had added his mobile phone number to the foot of the email, but despite my burning curiosity, I was reluctant to use it so soon. What I really needed to do was acquire today's edition of the local paper and find out what I'd said in that interview...or perhaps what the delicious journalist had quoted me as saying.

Five minutes later, I was standing in front of a street vendor, a man who looked as if he'd last washed during the Falklands conflict, and handing over a quid in exchange for a single copy of the Telegraph and Argus. Pacing away a few yards, I halted on a street corner and started flicking through the pages, slowing only once I'd neglected all the important news — middle east unrest, stock market volatility, mass government spending cuts; there was also some material about this weekend's city mela — until I reached the feature about plain old me.

I was very familiar with the photo the journalist had snatched from Oxford's website — not a bad picture, I thought; I did at least look amusedly distinguished — but more interested in what the text might offer. I quickly scanned it, snatching at the opening biographical information and soon getting to the meat of the matter. And then, following a necessarily brief account of my academic work (readers certainly wouldn't wish to be harried by jargon), I saw what my latest contactor must have read earlier today, before sending me a communication about something resonating with him:

"Despite all his important research, let's not suggest that Dr. Parker doesn't have a playful side. Indeed, during this short trip back to Bradford, he'll be looking into a spooky episode in our region's history. The felachnids, ancient

creatures with yellow eyes as well as limbs and heads that turn the wrong way, are supposed to originate in North Yorkshire. We sincerely hope Dr. Parker doesn't chance upon any of these entities while staying in the area!"

At that moment, while looking up from the name "Sara Edgeley" inscribed below the article, I spotted a man in dark glasses standing across the road. This reminded me of the guy I'd noticed yesterday in the pub, after John Marsh had discussed what he'd recently seen, and I experienced similar unease about my inability to decide where this person was staring. He might be glancing elsewhere — his body was tilted slightly away, facing the city hall nearby — or he might be looking at me. It wasn't even a bright day; a chaos of cloud hung low over Bradford, threatening all kinds of inclement intrusions. Why would anyone need shades in such a climate?

He could be blind, of course, which meant I had nothing to worry about. Nevertheless, while pacing away from the spot, holding the newspaper in one hand and my phone in the other, I observed the figure in my peripheral vision, wondering whether his now blurred form might start to follow. It didn't appear to, which came as a great relief, and after rounding a corner to enter the street in which my hotel was located, I finally made that call.

SEVEN

What would people reading the article think of me? More worryingly, how would John Marsh respond if he saw a copy of today's newspaper? In my experience, the Telegraph and Argus reached many homes in the city, and just then, I stupidly believed that any pride I might enjoy as a high achiever who'd been born here had been scuppered for life. "Eminent academic believes in supernatural beings," I imagined people whispering around me, even following me south back down the rail network to Oxford, where colleagues would make me a laughing stock. My career would be over, reputation in tatters...but then, while taking a taxi to the address given to me by the man who'd emailed earlier, I got a grip on myself.

My main concern should be the trust I'd betrayed after an old friend had shared an experience which had obviously rattled him. I hadn't identified the man by name, but even so, it felt like a shitty thing to do, an untypical oversight on the part of someone usually so conscientious. For some reason, I also believed I'd let down Glenn, my late younger brother. The connection was nebulous at best, but there the sensation stood anyway.

I overcame such foolishness by staring out of the taxi's passenger-seat window, observing the suburbs rushing by. The driver beside me was Asian and unsurprisingly uncommunicative; I imagined his English was limited to street-names, pubs and local attractions, all vocational necessities. But that was okay, because I didn't feel like talking anyway. I was taken rather by the transformation that had occurred in this part of Bradford, to the near south of the city, which used to be populated by mills built during the Industrial Revolution and once involved in the failed wool trade. Now many of these aged, listed buildings had been regenerated, becoming kitschy modern apartments for well-to-do employees working nearby, or even in Leeds with its greater share of big-time investment.

This was certainly an improvement. It had always been

dismaying to see so many of these once grand properties with innumerable broken windows and moss growing on their walls, even though I'd kind of grown up with such sights, as if they were the air I'd breathed or the wallpaper of my youth. The dwellings had since been smartened up, with glossy facades and allocated parking bays, gated boundaries and CCTV surveillance. Such security devices perhaps reflected tensions inherent in these locations, relatively close to communities known for high levels of poverty and all the social problems associated with that.

It was in one of these converted mills that Peter Richards lived, the latest informant in my erratic attempt to learn about the so-called felachnids. My telephone conversation with this man had been brief and to the point, but I'd hung up knowing one troubling thing: here was someone else who'd experienced a visitation from creatures whose appearance and behaviour seemed to fit the profile I'd defined in the newspaper feature − yellow eyes, impossible limbs, and necks that twisted right the way round.

Or rather, his wife had experienced this. Indeed, by the time I'd negotiated access to what turned out to be a swanky third-floor apartment in a fine building boasting an original chimney as a unique characteristic, it was her I mainly spoke to.

The Richards appeared to be an affluent couple in their early thirties, even though Peter (a stockbroker by trade, who mainly worked from home; he'd told me this much during brief introductions) had explained that his wife − Olive − had recently suffered a breakdown, when a troubled relationship with her mother had ended with the older woman's death. Olive was therefore vulnerable, and although Peter had first suspected that the story she'd told him the day after he'd returned from London on business had been a pill-induced delusion, reading the article about me in the local paper had made him question this conclusion. Because the two descriptive accounts had shared an uncanny resemblance.

All of this the man had told me in the entrance hallway, and when I was shepherded through to a large, plush lounge with much chunky, stylish furniture, I finally got to meet Mrs. Richards — or rather, Olive (as she insisted on me calling her). She was quite charming, and if not for my existing knowledge, I mightn't have guessed how unstable she presently was. So much can be achieved with medication these days.

Nevertheless, as she started talking at my casual invitation, what else could I think but that she was sicker than even her husband had led me to believe?

"It happened a few nights ago," she explained, pushing back long, blonde hair from her narrow face. "I awoke in the early hours, my head pounding. With the number of tablets I take at the moment, I'm surprised I get any sleep at all, but I usually manage to nod off at about ten, especially when Peter is away.

"Anyway, on this occasion, I thought I'd heard something. At first, still half-asleep, I imagined this was my husband, going to the bathroom or still up working, the way he often is, bless him. But then I remembered: I was alone in the apartment. And there was now definitely a sound coming from elsewhere.

"I got up and crossed the bedroom. I was dressed in only a nightgown. It was pitch-dark. The windows on this side of the building give on to empty land without any lights, and although we have lamps situated on the property's exterior walls, they all go off at midnight. So the only help I had while moving was what little moonlight fell through the curtains.

"But that turned out not to matter. As soon as I entered the hallway, I heard that noise again, like a repeated plastic clacking. It sounded like someone tapping something manmade — a tub of some description, but what sense did *that* make? All I did know was that it was coming from the room to my right, my husband's office which presently had its door shut. But...but if someone was in there, how had they got inside? I couldn't figure it out, even though I was now fully awake. Then I turned the handle.

"When I stepped forwards once the door was open, I felt a draught of cold air strike my face. I suffer hot flushes from my pills, and weirdly, despite being terrified, this sensation came as a relief, lending me courage as I advanced further into the room. But that...that was when I saw *it*.

"My legs turned to mush. The thing was sitting at Peter's desk in a swivel chair, working on his PC with its back to me. But when it heard me arrive, it turned immediately and gave a...a savage *hiss*. Honestly, it was the worst sound I've heard in my life — like a combination of some snake and an aggressive cat. And its eyes — oh God, its *eyes*. Even though there was little light here, they appeared *bright yellow*, like the distant headlamps of some approaching lorry, whose driver was drunk at the wheel. *Very* drunk. Because when the...the *thing* rose from the chair, sending it spinning on its hydraulic pole, its whole body seemed to *lose its structure*. One second it stood there, just like the young man it otherwise resembled — wearing a shirt, pants, shoes — and the next it had *changed*, altering its shape, with its...its limbs flipping backwards in the wrong direction, until it seemed to... well, to move across the room for the window, but not the way you or I would do so, rather *cat*-like, or maybe like a *spider*, the arms and legs bending over the creature's body, allowing it to crawl and slink at the same time, scrabbling across the carpet and then slightly up one wall, as if defying gravity.

"It was then that I noticed that the curtains were parted, and the window beyond them wide open. That accounted for the draught I still felt, and must be how the thing had entered our property. It was certainly how it left, its hissing bulk escaping through the gap below the sash, crawling out on limbs as...as pliable as rubber.

"As you know, Dr. Parker, we're on the third floor, but that damned creature just pushed right out, as if height and all the damage that might befall the likes of us were of no consequence. But that makes absolute sense, doesn't it? I mean, it had somehow overcome all the building's security systems to enter our apartment in the first place...hadn't it? *Hadn't* it, Peter?"

By this time, the woman had become quite distressed, adrenalin arising from her vivid recollections having roused her to great articulacy and hurried speech. Then her husband took her in his arms; he obviously cared a lot for her, and when, moments later, he accompanied her elsewhere — to their bedroom, I guessed — I could only begin to come to terms with the events I'd just heard about. But I didn't get far at all; as little as a few minutes after his departure, Peter Richards returned.

He told me he'd put Olive to bed; doctor's orders had decreed that, on long-term sick leave from her job in marketing, she must get as much rest as possible and avoid agitation. However, in light of such recent, troubling episodes, she and her husband had decided to share their problem with me. And I soon learnt there was more to tell.

Peter steered me through to his home-based office, the site of the frightening incident his wife had just related. At first, I thought he was about to ask me to conduct some kind of forensic examination,

41

as if my doctorate qualified me for any and all technical tasks, but then he sat at his desk to switch on his PC — the one the alleged felachnid had used before being caught at its crime.

Minutes later, Peter had logged onto what appeared to be his online trading account, a site whose facilities allowed him to pay for this fine pad. I'd done a bit of market dealing myself, mainly buying and selling specialist funds, paying handsome fees to managers who'd made me a decent return on investments over the last decade — certainly enough to ensure a happy eventual retirement. But I wasn't in this guy's league. He briefly showed me his complex portfolio, all high yielding "blue chip" stock and zippy smaller companies. He had about £200,000 in his cash account alone. I exhaled sharply, beginning to see what had been so appealing to a potential thief.

But this was a *supernatural creature* I referred to. Indeed, by now, I'd seriously begun to entertain the notion that the felachnids were *real*. Oh, I know, I know; it goes against every rational principle I professed to uphold in my academic discipline. But I was also committed to the scientific method, to evidence supporting hypotheses and how, in the absence of falsification, even implausible theories must stand. In short, I now had plenty of information in favour of the creatures' existence, and little, other than my wobbling scepticism, to refute it.

Peter Richards went on to tell me what he'd discovered after finding his wife in such a miserable state when he'd arrived home from London the day after her disturbing experience: £2,000 missing from his trading cash account.

"What do you mean *missing*?" I asked, still struggling to wrap my skull around all the new material I'd acquired that evening. "How can anybody get cash out of an e-platform?"

More to the point, how can a fucking cat-spider in human form do so? I truly wanted to ask this question, but somehow resisted and then awaited a reply from Peter.

Which came promptly: "He, it, whatever the thing was transferred the sum to a specific person named on the outgoing transaction."

This struck me as promising, but now another matter troubled me. "Hold on a moment," I said, feeling like some crime-scene investigator, suspecting everyone until they could be declared innocent. "How was he...how was *it* able to access your account?"

"I make a point of shredding every piece of paper that leaves this building and never talking to strangers on the phone. But what with her recent illness, my wife hasn't always been so vigilant. I don't know whether that creature rummaged in the rubbish outback or got Olive to reveal some vital information during a call, but whichever way they managed it, the intruder gained access to my log-in details."

"Okay. I see." I wasn't finished with my interrogation, however. Pressing the man a bit, I said, "But if they had this information, why break in *here*? Why not just access your funds via *any* PC?"

Peter told me about his security measures, how, manipulating so much money on a daily basis, he'd had complex software installed which restricted access to his platform to *this* computer, as well as his iphone for trading while travelling. The burglar, perhaps having tried and failed to use the access data elsewhere, had clearly been aware of this.

That presupposed a level of knowledge and sophistication that made me feel deeply uncomfortable — just how advanced had the felachnids become since their early, primitive days taunting mere villagers? — but then I returned to the task at hand.

"Whatever happened, all this makes it a criminal matter," I said, looking unblinkingly at the man. "May I ask why you haven't been in touch with the police?"

He glanced back at me, eyes narrowing. Then he smirked slightly. "We're both men of the world, aren't we, Dr. Parker. I mean, we can be discrete when we need to be, right?"

"Well, yeah," I replied, but didn't feel comfortable doing so. After all, observe what I'd done with the last private information with which I'd been entrusted, the first piece of evidence in this case provided by my old friend John Marsh.

Nevertheless, I listened as my latest informant shared his furtive secret. It turned out that he wasn't keen on any form of authority "sniffing around" his financial affairs. A small matter of unpaid capital gains tax and some sleight-of-hand "shuffling of cash" had been enacted during this financial year, and he'd been "loath to trouble all those nice, overworked people at Her Majesty's Revenue and Customs".

Well, none of that was anything to do with me and I was happy to stay out of it. But when Peter went on to provide the name and bank details of the person who'd received the relatively modest sum of money which someone — or perhaps some*thing* — had taken from him, I was immediately re-engaged and now determined to undertake the next stage of my ever-darkening investigation.

EIGHT

We planned to carry out the sting the following morning, after I'd tracked down the recipient of that sizeable quantity of cash.

One thing troubled me about the stolen £2,000, but that evening it failed to coalesce in my exhausted mind. It had been a long day and I was ready for bed. I had Peter Richards' mobile number, and after promising to be in touch as soon as I'd acquired more information (I knew a useful trick from conducting research with local authorities and the like), I returned to my hotel to catch some much-needed sleep.

My dreams that night were stark and oppressive, involving dark woods in which ambient eyes gazed at me while foliage shuffled, heralding the arrival of... But each time my flustered mind tried transforming these observers into visual form, the attempt failed, leaving just a fragmented image of my late brother, his face drained of blood.

I hadn't seen Glenn when he'd died — he'd been out partying in a nightclub — but his so-called friends had later described his overdose, before a coroner had made matters official. He'd died with his eyes wide open, they'd told me, and however much I'd tried suppressing this thought for months afterwards, I'd rarely been able to sleep without seeing those two haunted peepers, suggesting a tormented child trapped inside a young man's body.

When I awoke, very much located in Bradford, I again speculated about what had driven my brother to prolonged drug use while I'd pursued the world of knowledge and thought. Perhaps these had both been survival mechanisms...but survival from *what*? Depression, maybe — the natural consequence of enjoying sheltered upbringings in such a punishing location, like kittens cocooned in baskets amid a realm of tooth and claw? Soon the city's rough *mores* had invaded our lives, during edgy days at comprehensive schools, and later in the pitiably depleted jobs market. But I'd pulled away, got free, escaped. My younger brother, lacking my innate intelligence and conscientious application, had stayed where he was. And now he was dead — had been for twenty years. It *still* cut me up.

Once I'd showered and dressed, however, I realised I had a more pressing matter to attend to at the moment. It was now seven o'clock and I was unlikely to make a Friday morning breakfast downstairs. Instead I powered up my laptop, checked only perfunctorily for email (there were none of any significance), and then got down to the task I'd promised Peter Richards the previous evening.

As an academic conducting regular research with the public, I had a university-based account with a complex search engine, affiliated to the electoral register, which allowed me to locate particular people according to their name, gender, age, address, and some other demographics. In this case, I had the guy's moniker — Andrzej Kowalski, the recipient of the bank transfer from Peter's PC — and I was hoping Bradford didn't have such a large Polish community.

My best guess was that this guy — or possibly somebody associated with him — had discovered the Richards' log-in details from unshredded rubbish in the bins behind that converted apartment block. I could well imagine those *things* prowling among such refuge, seeking advantage in the manner described by my informant in Nathen — friendly Arnold — during my recent trip north.

Now they, or at least one of them, had taken to thieving, cross-wiring couples and neighbours in a way that could induce paranoia. What might Peter Richards have thought after arriving home to find money missing from his account? That his currently deluded wife, who knew his platform access data, had made the transaction? And how would a more dishonourable man, one who loved his spouse less, have dealt with that? How much damage might a person cause such a poor, sick woman?

Much of this was speculation, and something still didn't quite add up, but then I pushed it all to the back of my mind, hoping to identify the home location of our dear friend Andrzej Kowalski.

Five minutes later, I'd tracked down a promising candidate, one of only two identically named people in this administrative area (the other was based miles north in the market town of Skipton and seemed unlikely to be our man). The guy lived in nearby Manningham, less than ten minutes' drive away, and after jotting down the address, I gave Peter Richards a call and suggested that we might have located his thief. He promised to arrive at my hotel in less than an hour, and by God, if he didn't prove true to his word.

By ten o'clock that morning, we approached the street I'd detected via the search engine. My temporary colleague — my present co-researcher — seemed both anxious and vengeful. I sensed that he was less concerned about the money — which had amounted to just 1% of his trading cash — and more bothered by the fright the intruder had given his recovering wife. He knew something spooky was going on — I had the impression that he was as accepting as I'd become of Olive's description of their uninvited visitor — but was determined to put an end to any more activity of that pernicious stripe.

Once he'd parked up his predictable BMW, we got out and then advanced up the pathway of a squat terraced house, whose visible deprivation matched that of the street in which it was located to a depressing degree.

After I'd knocked at the front door, we received no immediate reply. That was hardly surprising, and just as Peter seemed to be about to suggest that we carry out a little bullish house-entry of our own, we heard footsteps from inside. This was hardly the quick stealthy tread of a creature equipped with limbs built for rapid mobility, but a kind of sluggish shuffle, more suggestive of someone intoxicated. That was when a suspicion lurking deep in my brain rose to the surface of consciousness.

Were the felachnids drug-takers? Was that why they needed quick, hard cash? Again, I recalled aspects of the tall tale Arnold had told me, how the entities, primed for devilment, had often used toxic substances as a way of tormenting their quarry, so many pitiable people trying to live decent lives. However, he'd also said they possessed an unusual capacity to tolerate such gear, while others around them tumbled and reeled.

But this was all nonsense, wasn't it? Surely I didn't now believe *everything* about this foolish myth...legend...call it what I would.

In any case, as the door started opening, I braced myself for the kind of action that, as a life-avoiding scholar, I was ill-prepared to handle. And then our target — the duplicitous Andrzej Kowalski — put in his long-awaited appearance.

He couldn't be much younger than eighty years old.

As the guy stood there, blinking in morning daylight, we noticed bruising on his face, the way he seemed to betray an embodied defensiveness, as if he'd been attacked lately and not with much restraint. He was dressed in the accoutrements of poverty, his garments unwashed, let alone ironed. He looked about as likely to scale a property up to its third floor as I could compose an opera.

Minutes later, we'd gained access to the house (hardly a masterstroke of negotiation; if we hadn't received permission, we might have simply barged inside), and were soon sat in a messy lounge, where a coffee table at the centre supported a number of items: dirty mugs, trays of unclean crockery, and — most significantly for our purposes — a number of bank account documents, including a withdrawal book. It didn't take an expert in fraudulent crime to figure out what had happened here.

Nevertheless, we spent a short while learning something about this elderly gentleman, who was indeed Polish and had been in the UK for thirty years. He'd once worked in the building game, a revelation that brought back unwanted thoughts about John Marsh and the way my current investigation had begun. But then I steered the guy on to the subject of money. He looked at me plaintively, those facial injuries a vibrant purple against his pale, cracked mask of skin. Moments later, his accent strong but English fair, he began talking.

"I and others like me in this area have been targeted for this kind of thing."

"*What* kind of thing?" Peter wanted to know, a tad more impatient than I was willing to be, and for a good reason, of course.

Andrzej Kowalski simply looked at us, each in turn. "I mean the young ones who wear hoods. They have no banks of their own and must use ours for their dealings. It happens maybe every few days."

Had I been right in suspecting this was all part of some mass drug operation? The man had mentioned other victims like himself — presumably similar older folk in the area — as well as "young ones" in the plural, implying multiple criminals. Just how widespread was this racket? And what involvement did the felachnids have in it?

I found it difficult to believe I'd been reduced to such foolhardy speculation in as few as two days; I'd left Oxford early-week, a respected empirical scientist. Nevertheless, impulse and a commitment to an evidence-based methodology drove me on. And that was when I asked, "Could you tell us something about the person who — I'm presuming, of course, but your injuries suggest this — who forced you to withdraw illegally transferred money from your account?"

The aged Pole glanced down at his bank documents, scattered uselessly across his table. Maybe he thought he had nothing left to lose, which had prompted him to let Peter and me inside. After entry, I'd introduced my colleague as a victim of similar criminal activities. If the thugs who'd done this to Andrzej Kowalski — *cat-spiders*, by Christ; yellow-eyed, elastic-limbed freaks — had threatened worse if he reported them, that might be why he'd decided to speak to us. In the absence of formal authorities, perhaps he thought we could help. Indeed, he soon spoke again.

"I haven't seen much of them. They — sometimes one, other times quite a different youth — come round when they need help. Often I resist. That is when they beat me. Look."

He pointed to his contusions, the split lip and swollen eyes. Hadn't neighbours noticed this, calling for assistance on his behalf? But then I recalled the state of the area, and realised how little folk probably cared around here — either that or they were too afraid.

Even so, I — maybe betraying a pampered, pseudo-middleclass naivety — found myself saying, "You really should go to the police, you know."

But the man only scowled, maybe even laughed a little. "They do nothing. Same as the newspaper. Where is such crime reported? Nowhere — never."

I sighed and then waited for our informant to go on.

Soon he did.

"The youths — they wear hoods most of the time, as I said earlier. I don't see their faces often, and when I do..." — the man paused a moment, as if his next words disturbed him, as well they should. After all, I knew what he was about to add — "...when I do, their *eyes* don't look right. They're too bright, somehow. Too...too..."

Yellow, I added mentally, but said nothing other than, "That's okay. You needn't go on." Then I glanced at my companion, another victim of these malicious creatures, these entities who preyed on the mentally ill in affluent settings, as well as elderly members of ethnic minority groups in less able circumstances. The felachnids. A breed of perverted *things* unable to integrate into conventional society, just as my Nathen informant had suggested. Looking the way they did, they were unable to get jobs, let alone bank accounts to pay salaries into. That was why they acquired virtual money from people like Peter Richards, turning it later into cash by forcing vulnerable people such as Andrzej Kowalski to withdraw the funds from their local branches.

There was also an element of the creatures' trickster nature here, playing off one social group against another. It may be a complicated procedure, but this was a lot more menacing than simply stealing and selling on jewellery or other pricey goods. And it would certainly maximise racial tensions in the city's volatile mixed communities, with one group possibly suspecting another of foul play, or at least using these episodes — as I knew extreme factions in any of them tended to — as excuses to do so.

Nevertheless, something troubled me about this conclusion, and when I decided it was time for Peter and me to leave, I stood and thanked the older man for his time and help. I finished by saying, "If there's anything else you can think of that might help us deal with this problem, could you let us know?"

I'd been about to offer him my university calling card — maybe a risky move, maybe not — when the guy stood, knees certainly not betraying the kind of flexibility his exploiters boasted, and grabbed one of my arms. At first, I thought he was seeking support in maintaining his balance, but then he moved his head closer to mine, so that I could observe every one of his pitiful wounds. Seconds later, he whispered into my ear.

"I remember what they wear. Tracksuit tops, I think they're called. But these...these are different. They bear a logo."

That was hardly surprising; most youngsters these days were found bedecked in such stuff, all besmirched by the puerile insignia of multinational sportswear companies, stripes or swishes or pumas.

But then Andrzej Kowalski started running his finger against my jacketed chest, first down at a leftwards diagonal, then right at ninety degrees, and finally up a bit, but not far at all. He'd just inscribed an L-shape, tipped on its side, with a tiny foot pointing inwards.

And I immediately knew how I was supposed to picture this.

NINE

As we drove away, I spotted a youth in sunglasses standing on the corner of the street. It was again an inclement autumn day, cloud heavy in the sky and a threat of rain pinching at the flesh. Why would anyone wear shades in such a climate? Otherwise, this boy — maybe sixteen years old — looked like any youth we might see in such an area, dressed in casual clothing, limbs as orthodox as any person's.

Nevertheless, when we pulled away as he walked up towards the house we'd just visited, I refused to glance into the car's side mirror. I was so wired from what we'd learned from Andrzej Kowalski that the sight of the dude's face pointing backwards while his body moved forwards would probably break me apart.

Back in the city centre, a thought crystallised in my mind, forcing me to speak to the presently silent Peter Richards. "We need to go back to your place."

"You mean, *you*, too? But why?"

The issue bothering me since yesterday had now developed wings and was trying to get off the ground. "Let's just say I have a hunch."

"Do you want to tell me about it?"

I'd have to before long, so why not immediately? With an apprehensive exhalation, I said, "Since I learnt about the money you had stolen — that two-grand — a question has been nagging me. And it's simply this. Why not take *more*?"

"More money, you mean?"

"Yes, why didn't they take a whole batch of it? You have plenty in your account. So why did the thief limit himself — *it*self — to only a tiny part of the lot?"

Peter had already steered away from the direction of my hotel, heading south towards his own gaff. Then he said, "Transferring much more than a couple of K can raise alerts at banks. I know automated machines detect potential money laundering activities, especially if it goes to someone with no previous involvement with the account holder."

"I had considered that, actually," I said, and wasn't lying; I'm worldly, me. But then I got serious again. "Okay, here's what I reckon. The thing — the creature — the felachnid..." — Christ, was I really saying all this? Yes, I guessed I was — "...it was scared away first time, but only after it had completed its modest transaction. In hindsight, however, it might have thought — no offence, mate, but this is surely true — that there's just a vulnerable woman in this particular property, which makes the place much less risky than others it's violated. So why not *go back there*? Why not treat that account as a nice, big cash cow, to be milked whenever more ill-gotten funds are required?"

The driver thought for a moment, face registering realisation. I could tell he understood where I was going with this: a little night-time vigil, an overnight wait for the intruder to return. Then, eyes brighter than I'd seen them since our first meeting, he responded.

"You think we should lie in waiting for it, don't you?"

I nodded. "Andrzej Kowalski said the things have bothered him and others he's aware of every few days. Which means they're likely to try again soon, maybe even tonight. It's got to be worth a try."

Peter thought for a moment, but then said, "Okay, I'm willing to give it a go."

"Good," I replied, now happy with developments. "So am I."

"Yes, let's wait up for the little bastard and then rip its fucking head off."

I was less attracted to this possibility, but said nothing as the vehicle accelerated, charging towards that smartly converted mill. In any case, my mind had now shifted to another matter, one I considered as serious as the missing loot. I thought back to what our Polish informant had claimed about himself and similar others in the area being targeted for financial misdemeanours.

Similar others. Old folk battered and bruised. The elderly accessing bank branches wearing bloody makeup and not raising the suspicions of either staff or pedestrians. This troubled me deeply. How had the police not become involved? Why hadn't the newspaper been informed? Did local journalists spend most of their time interviewing (let alone screwing!) relatively insignificant people like me? What the hell was going on in this sprawling mess of a city, with its incongruous proximity to so much glorious countryside...and the demons which had possibly bred there, now seeking a far larger community to corrupt?

TEN

As we pulled into the lengthy road in which the Richards lived, I saw a large advertisement on a bus shelter for the city's multicultural mela festival, due to take place the following day. With all my frantic investigations during the last forty-eight hours, I'd pushed this event to the back of my mind, and although I still planned to attend, I knew I presently had a more crucial concern to address.

At the sight of the tall, ex-operational chimney on one side of the transformed building, my heart rate stepped up several notches, wondering whether tonight — it was only noon at the moment, but just a few hours short of darkness — I'd finally lay eyes on one of the mythical felachnids.

With three convincing independent accounts of these invasive creatures, I no longer doubted that they — or certainly something closely resembling them — existed. This conclusion was based on logic, after all; however absurd it seemed, if no evidence could be found to invalidate it, a theory must be held as true. Hadn't

Sherlock Holmes said something to this effect — once maybe, in a fictional book, which possibly had as little to do with everyday life as my present enquiry related to my brother's death?

Nevertheless, as Peter and I entered the building and then spent the afternoon preparing for the possibility of a second intrusion from something beyond our brains' capacity to assimilate, I began thinking that this case had become a way for me to exorcise Glenn's ghost, shaking off a residual sense of guilt. I didn't actually believe I should have been in that nightclub at the time of his demise; that sort of "what if" thinking was far from healthy. It was rather that I reckoned I might have done something different during our youths, something that could have made the impact of difficulties in later life less of a shock to his system. Glenn hadn't got on well with the work the likes of he, myself and John Marsh had ended up doing. The building game was a tough trade, full of taunting twats and embittered spouses, each taking out their familial tensions and financial responsibilities on anyone who fitted the bill — on anyone who showed vulnerability.

My brother, on the surface quite a wily guy, was as fundamentally sensitive as me. He simply hid it better than I, but you know, that's not always a positive thing. While my weaknesses were all too apparent, his were driven down deep, as if they didn't exist at all. And when I'd eventually fled to get an education and to make sense of the whole mess involved in surviving this unforgiving world, he'd remained on a less noble path — the drugs in which we'd all dabbled as teens — until he'd fallen clean off the cliff.

I should have done more; I really should. But just what, I hadn't been sure. I'd probably know *now*, what with the lengthy row of letters after my name and possessing so much bullshit knowledge of psychology. But I hadn't known *then*, had I? That was the tragedy; that was *always* the tragedy. Knowledge comes long after you need it, and you only learn how to avoid mistakes by making them in the first place. But then it was too fucking late. I was Glenn's bigger brother, and he'd died on my watch. How cruel can life get?

Hell, I was feeling low that evening, as the sky slipped from grey to greyer to black. The moon was a vicious hook among a field of indifferent stars; whatever clouds there'd been earlier had blown away, as if by a God keen to observe what some of His more malevolent unearthly creations were about to enact in such a lowly place, a city rife with anxieties, where real people already had quite enough integrative problems to deal with.

Just then, as Peter and I took up our previously agreed stations in different parts of the apartment (Olive, the man's wife, had been persuaded to visit friends, who'd agreed to let her stay the night), I recalled my informant Arnold's account of the creatures' possible origin, travelling from beyond the stars on a meteorite of sorts, which suggested they weren't even humans, despite closely resembling us.

From an evolutionary perspective, that was quite plausible; presumably a similar ecosystem in another world would exert the same kind of adaptive pressures on a species, leading to identical sensory apparatus, with a head uppermost, limbs top and bottom, and a bipedal method of mobility. Opposable thumbs might have developed as a result of tool use, just as they had in homo sapiens, and those additional attributes — the yellow eyes, flexible limbs, necks that twisted further than human muscles allowed — may have emerged from particular aspects of that alien realm, maybe less vibrant sunlight, a more intricate landscape, and a higher number of predators, necessitating 360-degree orientation. Maybe this final factor — fear of being rendered extinct — was the reason they'd fled their true home, a limited number falling in a single, secluded spot in Yorkshire as long as a millennium ago, before modern surveillance could detect their arrival.

Maybe, perhaps. Most of this was reckless speculation, but I entertained it anyway; it passed time between now and...well, when *they* might arrive.

And at about eight o'clock, they did.

Or rather, one of them did, possibly the same as the previous visitor, who'd pocketed a nice bonus that day. What the things were using this cash for, I could only guess at, but as Peter and I heard that entity rattling the man's office window, we left our positions — he in the hallway, myself in the lounge — and came together outside the door, waiting for the felachnid to enter.

Indeed, what else *could* this be? We were on the third floor, after all. Our plan was to let the thief settle down to its illegal work, using those purloined log-in details to access Peter's stock market account. Such systems are built for speed, the owner had told me during our car journey that morning; as traders required funds exactly where and when they needed them at any given time, there were no transaction delays. This clearly appealed to the felachnids, something else implying a level of furtive knowledge way above the norm.

Christ, this new breed of the monsters were no bungling amateurs; they appeared organised and focused, all of which had started to worry me. At first, I thought they were simply after what a lot of young folks these days crave: drugs. But that didn't correspond with my Nathen-based informant's story, did it? The things were more pernicious that that; they wanted to destroy communities, playing one person off against others, and vice versa. And so what *were* they up to in the ethnic and economic powder-keg that was the city of Bradford?

All these thoughts would have to be reserved for later; right now, I had a burglar to catch. When Peter and I made our move, we did so quickly, me opening the door and then hurtling forwards to cut off exit to the window, while he tried grappling with the beast, however dangerous that might be. But I knew the man had a score to settle; his fragile wife hadn't slept well lately, and Peter had related this directly to her recent fright.

Once I'd crossed to the far wall, where curtains billowed up in a gust of seasonal wind, I turned to see the other two sizing up to each other. At first glance, the creature — the felachnid — was almost disappointing, looking like nothing other than a city youth, dressed in standard sports-gear, the kind you might see on any street corner or council estate in urbanised areas.

But then, its body recoiling from the potential threat presented by the retributive homeowner, the thing switched its vicious gaze my way.

Its eyes were like pools of yellow acid.

While talking to the lady of the house last night, I'd become aware of a new element characterising these sick entities: the sadistic hissing sound they made. That happened on this occasion, too, the fleshy red mass of a tongue appearing briefly between its thin lips. And now a further attribute became apparent: their smell. This was a fetid odour, like a cat on furtive heat, the pheromone-packed scent sweeping across the small room, rendering my feelings edgy and strange, as if an animal was about to seize me, and for no honourable reason.

I recoiled at once, watching the swivel chair the figure had just vacated turn in front of the Richards' already activated PC. There was no website onscreen; the felachnid hadn't got very far before we'd arrested its progress. Maybe that might make it madder. But it looked pretty mad anyway.

Peter made a move for it; the thing leapt backwards, clattering a printer off the desktop. Then I joined in, trying to form a pincer manoeuvre with my vengeful companion, herding the fucker into one corner. But that was when something incredible occurred.

Trapped by our advance, the felachnid, eyes blazing as bright as distant suns, rolled back on its haunches, coiling like a cat about to strike some ineffectual quarry — a mouse, maybe, or a common garden bird. And then its limbs *bent the wrong way*. One moment the thing stood as we did, the natural contours of a human body unremarkably sustained; the next it defied conventional anatomy, certainly for the species it mimicked, and it leapt forwards, darting away, up one wall alongside the open window and then briefly across the ceiling, falling behind us near the office door, hurtling through, scurrying along the hallway and finally out towards the apartment's main entrance.

We gave chase immediately, turning quickly, despite our combined bewilderment, a sensation registered by one exchanged glance. *This is real*, that gaze communicated, and just then, I recalled that Peter hadn't previously seen the creature, that only his wife had. This was a new experience for both of us, but to some degree, we'd already accepted the truth prior to the event, and that helped us get on.

We rushed into the hallway, in full pursuit of the creature. By this time, the felachnid had got the front door open (we hadn't thought to lock it, expecting the intrusion from elsewhere) and was, to judge by footsteps skittering beyond the threshold, racing down the communal passage, almost certainly heading in a haphazard way for the staircase down three flights and then mercifully out of the building.

Not hesitating for even a moment, Peter and I rushed out of the apartment, joining the pursuit at a pace my ageing body was ill-prepared for. Soon sweat ran into my eyes, distorting my vision, and I'd like to think this accounted for the image up ahead, a decidedly human figure, dropped to all fours, racing across the plush carpets of this converted mill like some oversized mammal. But even the wildest animals lacked its slipshod musculature, its skeletal dexterity. The way its limbs appeared to bend, like multi-jointed instruments, was astonishing to observe, even though moisture continued marring my sight. Through a sheen of smudges, I saw the entity bounce off the walls of the stairwell, scuttle momentarily on ceilings, scrabble like the insect it now resembled through a new doorway on the last level.

If the largest earthbound spiders could expand a hundredfold and be cross-fertilised with human DNA, it might look something like this. The thing was hideously creepy, and I wanted to be sick. But I somehow kept moving, through that last opening and out into the place's main lobby, with which I was familiar from my two visits here.

At that moment, luck on our side for once, somebody outside approached the main entrance, which was operated by either a combination code box or an intercom system beside it. This woman was clearly a tenant, because after hacking in four digits (I'd used the alternative entry method), she paced up close to the doors, waiting for them to unlock. She was about twenty-five years old, exquisitely dressed, and seemed blithely unaware of the horror-show into which she was about to step.

But as it turned out, that didn't matter. By now, the felachnid, still vilely transformed into some kind of cat-spider-human hybrid, started scuttling the other way, along a new arm of the building, an extensive corridor leading to one of the preserved original features: that chimney I'd observed from the exterior.

Peter and I, both gasping for breath, followed.

By the time I reached the end of that passageway, however, I was alone. Driven now by adrenalin, I was unable to stop and turn to see what had become of my temporary partner, why he'd fallen behind. I was too busy assessing the scene up ahead.

The base of the chimney had been exposed, leaving an impressive stone walkway beneath it, enabling residents to walk to and fro through fabricated arches on each side. It was a smart feature, a unique selling point, and I could imagine why young, trendy types, with money to spend and the desire to do so, wanted to live here. The lower lip of the chimney's circular structure was about twelve feet off the ground, double my height, but that thing — that creature — that felachnid had entered the chute anyway. It must have gathered momentum while scurrying along the carpeted hallway behind me, sinking ever lower on those impossible limbs. Then it had clearly leapt off the ground, reaching one face of the wall stretching up, bouncing from that to the opposite side and then back again, using its complexly jointed arms and legs to enact a zigzag motion, right to the top of the chimney, maybe a hundred feet high. Indeed, amid my breathless panting, I could hear its hands and feet scuffling against the stone, as it repeatedly bounded across the ten-foot diameter of this improvised exit route.

Moments later, still looking into the shadows of that frightful throat, I felt fingertips upon my shoulder and then whirled at once. Peter stood there, looking similarly exhausted, but also quite triumphant.

"I know where it's headed," he said, holding up an object which had apparently been jettisoned during the chase.

By this time, the sounds of fleeing above had diminished to failing echoes and then to nothing at all. Even if we did run outside and try to catch the monster making its escape, we'd have little chance of doing so. It was too fast, too wily, too able.

But that was when my vision cleared enough for me to review what my newest friend brandished.

And just then, I felt more scared than I had at any point during all these unexpected events.

ELEVEN

What Peter had found on the ground floor was a folded piece of paper advertising the dubious charms of a nightclub situated in downtown Bradford. On the back was a handwritten symbol:

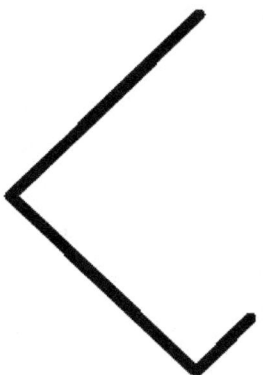

It certainly looked as if we'd tracked the felachnids to their local base.

As we took a taxi to this hothouse of carnal, illicit activity, I tried suppressing my deepest fears by worrying about a further development in the case of my new research subjects. If the creatures were numerous and appeared to operate from a particular venue, was their occupancy of the city permanent? Had they — or at least some of them — flocked from the north, that small village of Nathen, to cause unrest on a major scale?

Just then, my brain clogged with speeding thoughts and body tired from the hunt, I was unable to appreciate what the things were trying to achieve. Was this really just devilment at work, the petty goal identified by Arnold, an admittedly amateur local historian? Were the felachnids biologically programmed as a species to maximise others' duress? Did this amuse them? Or did they actually *consume* such misery, as if they were vicarious vampires feasting on relative unhappiness?

Something about this latest thought offered me leverage on the problem; it felt as if an understanding was germinating deep down, the way many of my theories begin, a stirring in the gut suggesting truth. In these situations, I usually returned to the world, seeking evidence to support my hunches, feelings, nebulous insights. And now I was determined that this study would be no different. To understand what my new subjects were up to, I required a full dataset. I needed to conduct a little ethnographic research in their natural habitat.

But to do that, I'd have to revisit the site of one of the worse things that had ever happened to me: the Charnel House nightclub where my brother had died.

As I've said, I wasn't with Glenn at the time, but I'd visited the place a few occasions prior to that and never again afterwards. It was a seedy joint, full of local players and acid queens. If it was drugs you were after, this was your one-stop shop. I recalled that any and all illegal substances could be grabbed from here: uppers, downers, poppers; smack, crack, pot; plentiful Es, if you please — the whole range, like some kind of heretical supermarket full of eager merchants and banging deals.

As our taxi pulled up in front of the spot, music boomed from its frontage, rendering shadows in the doorway alive with a promise of joy, and a couple of bouncers standing on either side all the more motionlessly imperious. Having paid the fare, we got out of the vehicle, myself not without a degree of trepidation, and then advanced upon the building, its low roof belying the vast dance-hall at its core. I remembered at once that this was an underground attraction, in just about every sense. You entered and then immediately descended a flight of stairs, if not even — temporarily, at least — down the evolutionary ladder.

The bouncers were sweet guys, letting us in with a nod and wink. After all, who could be more responsible than a couple of well-to-do middle-English aspirants like ourselves? We mightn't look like party animals, but we had money, and, maybe more than most clients here, needed to unwind at the end of a working week. As I'd paid for the taxi, Peter grabbed two entry passes and then we were away, plunging into hell, or rather, my own personal one.

But I tried keeping my mind on the task at hand. Little could be achieved by dwelling on past events I was unable to change, even if I did feel as if this visit back to my native environment, especially the way it seemed to be ending here, was some weird Freudian exorcism whose parameters were presently unidentifiable.

Thunderous music, like elephants stampeding, filled a room as large as a church. A manic congregation jittered and jived, their impossibly pliable bodies configuring new patterns of multicoloured light as we moved around the centre, headed for the bar on the far right. Whenever I glanced across at all the party people, looking of course for any suggestion of felachnids, I saw exposed flesh, tattoos aplenty, and faces writhing with chemically enhanced ecstasy. Although most appeared fluid of limb, none betrayed any tell-tale evidence of *that* particular characteristic, neither arms and legs flexing the wrong way nor faces looking too far over shoulders. There was a raw aroma of human perspiration, but that's all this was; any bestial consequences would occur later, between consenting adults.

We got our drinks — something short we could easily abandon, but which rendered us inconspicuous — and then started making our rounds. At one stage, while passing a bunch of Goth types, one turned and stared at me, revealing mismatching eyes — one green, the other orange. I was still wired from all the evening's events, and immediately imagined two yellow peepers gazing my way, but then I realised what was happening: the Goth wore contact lenses, a different one covering each unblinking iris. I quickly looked away, trying to steady my mounting anxieties.

In which part of this room had Glenn suffered his overdose? But no, I didn't want to think about that; it was both unhealthy and a hindrance to what I was attempting to achieve. When Peter and I reached another corner, incapable of making comments because the music — some kind of syncopated trance routine — was so loud, we simply exchanged nods which read: *Remain vigilant. Tap and point if you see anyone who fits our description.*

And then, just as the track on the sound system switched to something even more disarmingly raucous, we spotted one.

A felachnid.

Thriving in its new ecological niche.

The fact that all the creatures I'd encountered so far had been young men didn't surprise me. Even in an alien species, it might be the males who took the risks, doing most of the dirty work. Nevertheless, to survive as a group, procreation must be involved, which meant there had to be women, too — or rather, whatever this creepy race called their lady-folk, child-bearers, possibly even homemakers. But what kind of a private life, outside cheating and chiding, could these things have?

Witness this latest example, the way he handed over a small packet from an inside jacket pocket. My suspicions were first aroused by the fact that he wore shades — a pair of sunglasses indoors, and in such intermittent light — but then I noticed something even more damning: the symbol — that logo denoting their creed — stitched to the side of the hood wrapped around that deceptively adaptive neck. Maybe this had become their calling card, a message that "drugs were available here". Perhaps the city centre building site, the one on which my old friend John Marsh presently worked, was another unofficial drop-zone for toxic substances.

At any rate, the full story was finally falling into place: how the things stole from the affluent, used the vulnerable as cash depositories, and invested their ill-gotten loot in goods they spread around the community. They might be new to the game, lacking start-up funds. With any luck, Peter and I had latched on to them at this nascent stage.

The creatures were certainly ambitious. As far as I knew, Bradford was no different from others cities in that its prominent drug dealers would be the usual bunch of dangerous psychos with networks running all over the city. I imagined many belonged to non-native communities, but that's not a racist observation;

the simple truth was that such cultural disadvantage — ethnic penalties paid in the jobs market — drove people to less orthodox methods of achievements. That's a fact. Read your sociology.

Why the felachnids would want to muscle in on territory already occupied by the area's own breed of *agent provocateurs* puzzled me, however. If destabilisation was their goal, why didn't they just remain in whatever they'd claimed as their homes and gain vicarious delight from news reports, from plentiful stories about street fights, riots, and vandalism? From tales of muggings, fraud and burglary? Or from accounts of young men, with all their long lives ahead of them, taking a batch of shitty drugs and ending everything in what might even be called, with borderline paradoxicality, a wilful accident?

That thought got me going again, setting aside my drink and cutting directly across to the dealer with my companion in eager tow. And I'd just processed another troubling thought — one about a lack of reports in the local newspaper concerning crimes befalling the likes of Andrzej Kowalski, as revealed by the Pole — when we reached the foul fucker and, having just dealt with one customer, he turned to observe us through those dark, reflexive lenses.

There was no recognition in his body language, implying that this young guy wasn't the one we'd chased from the apartment block with that kitschy chimney. The realisation merely reinforced my notion that lots of the bastards were at work right now, possibly patrolling the whole city. But *what* was their purpose?

Then the guy — about my height, scrawny, skin pale in the ever-changing disco-light — spoke over the din, clearly expecting us to supplement aural distortions with a little lip-reading. "And what might you finely dressed fellas be after?"

If he suspected that we were plains-clothes police, he showed no sign of apprehension. His pockets probably full of gear, he simply gazed implacably back (as far as I could detect through those thick, black glasses) as I leaned slowly towards him.

"Not here," I said, my voice carried by determination; but soon I was right up close to one of his ears. "I'm a professional man with a reputation to uphold. It wouldn't be good for me to be seen buying, if you know what I mean. Can we go somewhere more private?"

Again, the man looked casual, as if he was used to handling both himself and any tricky situation that might arise. Indeed, he then hoisted one back-curled forefinger, suggesting we might follow him, across the rear of the huge room to a set of double doors. He went immediately through them; we followed. Now, the booming sounds tempered, we stood in a short passageway, leading to more doors right at the end: a Ladies and a Gentlemen.

Once inside the latter, having exchanged no further words in the relative quiet, we stood beside a row of toilet cubicles, each ostensibly unoccupied. The light here was cold and weak, and although my eardrums still trembled from the assault they'd suffered only moments earlier, I could at last focus on my goal.

Without a second's hesitation, both Peter and I, acting in intuitive unison, grabbed hold of the felachnid and shoved him violently into one of the cubicles.

As I kept hold of the thing, my colleague locked the door, trapping all three of us inside. By this time, the creature was jerking back and forth, hissing like a cat, limbs twisting and bending like those of some horrid insect — a spider maybe, one from the eeriest recesses of a benighted planet. At any rate, I managed not to let the entity slip away this time, and when Peter finally joined in, we had it captured.

That was when I began demanding fast answers.

"What the fuck *are* you?"

After all the inebriation we'd witnessed in the main part of this venue, it was surprising when the guy answered in a perfectly lucid voice.

"I'm exactly what you deserve, my friend. *All* of you."

He'd spoken so calmly, so clearly, that I was immediately put in mind of something else my Nathen-based informant had told me: how the felachnids possessed an unusual capacity to tolerate toxic substances, while others around them grew increasingly inebriated. At that moment, I recalled the youths with whom my brother had once hung out, each clearly boasting a greater capacity to absorb such powerful stuff. In fact, during some of my weaker moments, I'd sometimes believed *they'd* killed him, what with their idiotic masculine belief in the body's indestructibility and a juvenile need to enhance ego. Glenn had just been trying to keep up, fit in. But he'd failed, big style — the biggest of all.

By this time, that scent had returned, a heady combination of some sexed-up cat and a shitting insect. It was horrible, even worse than smells expected in a place like this, where an overworked toilet bowl was smeared with goo. But that was when I turned my attention back to the beast. Maybe I could use my senior age and the way I was dressed to my advantage, after all; it would mean bluffing, of course, but what the hell? The things played dirty, and so why shouldn't I?

"I know what you're carrying, man. So give me one good reason why I shouldn't arrest you."

The creature laughed out loud. "It's *much* too late for that, fella," he said, as if accepting the possibility that I was a covert policeman but not caring anyway.

Something about his response disturbed me — it had felt like a non sequitur, somehow — and I went quickly on, despite Peter beside me looking askance in my peripheral vision.

"Listen, pal, I want names of all your associates. Where they live. How many. The whole lot. You hear?"

Christ, if I now sounded like some clichéd American cop, my only excuse is that I'd watched too many crime shows as a 1970s kid. In any case, it made no difference. The young man only laughed some more.

"There's nothing you can do to stop it," he said, now actually sniffing at me, those glasses unmoved from his face. He continued twitching his nose, as if drawing in my scent and then analysing stimulants produced by this possibly enhanced sensory ability. "You're a fake, my man. Just as I am. My accomplices are similar, but I imagine you're aware of them. Anyway, whatever the truth is, the fact remains that *it* will happen anyway."

At that moment, I hesitated, looking to my left. Peter glared back, equally nonplussed. I'm convinced one of us seriously considered knocking off the guy's ridiculous shades, exposing his fiery yellow eyes to the fierce strip-lights above. But then we both turned back to him at once.

"*What* will happen?" I asked, with a feeling of fatality I hadn't experienced since I'd heard the terrible news about my brother, twenty years earlier.

And then the felachnid said only one word: "Mela."

TWELVE

That night, after returning to my hotel, I scrutinised the newspaper I'd bought recently and left open at the feature the stunning Sara Edgeley had run with me.

Christ, had all that happened only a few days ago? It seemed an age since she and I had done such sordid things in this room. In truth, my body still thrilled to her touch, but so much had occurred lately that I could be forgiven for thinking she'd never been here, that the startling sex we'd enjoyed had been just some kind of early-middle-aged wet dream.

As I turned the newspaper back to its front page, I felt the weight of my exploits beginning to take their toll. I wasn't young anymore; the energy which had once helped me haul bricks on a building site and then party all night was simply not there now. I'd have to go steady during what remained of my adventure, but the fact was that I must keep going.

Major problems were developing in this city, possibly even another breakdown of multicultural relations. Cross-ethnic unity was essential if certain fanatical elements of all races were to be challenged or even overcome. Particularly pernicious agents of hard-line groups were always waiting for a catalyst to spark off more protests, often even violent ones. Indeed, a sabotaged public event would provide an ideal excuse to hit the streets again, possibly burn them up and then clash with police in such a serious way that the damage — both concrete and communal — would take many more years to heal.

While paging through the Telegraph and Argus, I chanced upon articles about the activities of Muslim communities, as well as those of Hindus and other foreign groups. As Bradford ostensibly welcomed diversity, it was important for members of many religiously oriented organisations to live well together, even sharing their different *mores*. This was of course the virtue and appeal of the mela, an annual festival devoted to celebrating such varying social and spiritual perspectives.

Among few stories about crime clearly blighting the area — an observation reinforcing my concerns about the efficacy of local journalism — I spotted several articles concerning the forthcoming event, including news that it would be opened by a leading dignitary from the local authority, someone only months in post and unprecedentedly young. There were other features about bands performing, organised events, and — the key attraction, surely — the wide range of food available.

It all sounded tremendous, except for one nightmarish fact: *it was going to be ruined.* The felachnids, using this convenient public occasion during which a huge group of people — possibly as many as 100,000 — from a vast number of backgrounds would descend upon a park just outside the city centre, were about to ratchet up communal tensions to a wild degree.

THIRTEEN

The creature Peter and I had trapped the previous night in a public toilet had followed up its insidious threat with an unsightly display of snarling and writhing, to such a degree that, with mutually resigned nods, we'd simply set it free, opening the cubicle door and watching it stalk off without troubling even one of its complex limb-joints. Before exiting the bathroom, however, it had turned its savage face towards us, offering a final glance through those ridiculous sunglasses. But the body hadn't shifted at all, just kept on walking the other way, trailing the head pointed in the opposite direction.

That had been horrifying enough, but the thought of what it and its nefarious accomplices intended to do today was worse. My understanding of their plan was now clear: after accumulating sufficient dubious substances, using money stolen from fragile people, they'd spike the food of nations, causing mass mayhem, just the way my friend up north — the amateur historian Arnold — had suggested their distant antecedents once had in a much smaller place. Back then, the things had used ancient brews and potions, drawing upon such quaint ingredients as local mushrooms; but these days, options were far more volatile, including chemically enhanced materials that could induce every mood, from delight to rage.

I won no prize for guessing which human emotion the felachnids were likely to aim for.

After arriving early at the festival site, I wondered how the things had lived in the city for so long without being detected. They could hardly operate out of property; that presupposed some rental or purchase arrangement, and how could that be managed when they looked the way they did? Maybe the additional drugs they dealt — all the witchy concoctions the guy last night had clearly had available — provided extra funds to get by. They might live along alleys or under the rafters of abandoned property (hardly in short supply around Bradford), eking out their survival until the time arrived when they could cause the most communal damage.

This was surely a police matter, or perhaps that of a more

specialised authority. But what the hell was *I* supposed to do? I guessed my academic status might stand for something, but even so, the thought of turning up at some local station and sharing with officers what hearsay knowledge I'd acquired surely had disreputable implications. Yes, Peter Richards and his wife could provide corroboration, and possibly John Marsh, too, if he wasn't too pissed off about my betrayal of his trust. But time was too short, just as the dealer had claimed the previous evening. It was all going to happen *today*.

And so what did I hope to achieve by attending the site of this impending disaster? Did I tacitly plan to enact an "online" intervention, persuading the police presence at the event — it would surely have a sizeable one — that certain disruptive activities were underway? It was impossible to say; understandably, I hadn't slept very well and wasn't thinking too clearly.

What I did in the event was simply join the throng, a multicultural mass swarming towards a network of stalls, performance stands and eateries. It was a cool, dry day, and very bright. The air was filled with a heady mix of ethnic music, spicy scents and incessant chatter. Folk as old as anyone I'd ever met stood alongside people my own age, some younger, and also children darting back and forth, having one helluva time, as only they know how. As expected, there were quite a number of police patrolling the park's fields and lakeside, and under a large canopy, several important looking people stood waiting, each dressed in smart, formal garments. I imagined the newly appointed mayor was one of this gang, as well as councillors and upstanding members of various communities, many belonging to Asian or other Black groups.

The whole vision was a celebration of human possibilities, how multiple cultures could interact with joy, dignity and respect. But this only gave what I knew was about to happen even greater tragic force. I had no idea whether the many sources of food on display here — huge drums full of heated curry, tasty fried morsels, exotic drinks by the gallon — had already been spiked or that was still to occur. All I did know was that I must *do* something to stop people consuming any of it.

It was then that I spotted a mechanism by which this might be achieved.

At precisely the same time, I noticed the first person I suspected to be a felachnid. The youth, a woman on this occasion, was White-British and dressed in casual sportswear, including a pair of tell-tale shades clinging to her pale face. She might be about seventeen years old, and although she was the only female I'd seen possibly affiliated to this pernicious band, she forced me to speculate that the creatures at work here, in Bradford's city centre, were perhaps a new generation of the creed, a rebellious out-group, eager to travel far and wide. Indeed, might this operation — the corruption of a diverse location — be just a pilot study, ahead of more ambitious projects, in the UK, across Europe, even around the world?

I *had* to put a stop to this, if only for my own sense of well-being. Doing otherwise felt like a betrayal of Glenn. I'd done nothing to save my little brother, but might now do something to preserve the honour of our troubled hometown. In both cases, cursed drugs were involved, and that forced me to carry out what I surely must do next.

Turning back to Sara Edgeley, the journalist I'd just seen standing near the dignitaries' canopy, I started walking that way.

Now quite alone in my mission (Peter Richards had gone today to collect his wife from their friends, feeling that he'd contributed as much as he could to my enquiries), I reached the woman just as the mayor stepped up to a microphone, presumably to deliver the mela's welcoming introduction, declaring the festival open and announcing that all attractions — including so much uniquely seasoned food — were available to enjoy.

That meant nobody had eaten yet, and after taking Sara by one arm and tugging her aside, away from the group she'd stood alongside, I realised there was a chance to prevent the festival from starting. If the journalist had connections with the great and the good in the district, as suggested by her position up here among them, she might be able to help.

"*Dr. Parker,*" she said, with some degree of surprise; I wasn't sure I'd mentioned during our interview my plan to attend this event, but failed to see why she might find that unusual. "I didn't realise you were still in town."

She now sounded quite anxious, but I struggled to see why. Had she been tasked with making notes on this important day, with a view to composing a report later? After all, she was a writer on culture and leisure in the local newspaper. Whatever the truth was, those unforgettable blue eyes flashed in the fierce morning light as, several yards to one side of us, the mayor began speaking.

His voice boomed across the now attentive mass. Here were Pakistanis and Indians, Bangladeshis and Chinese. Lord alone knew how many other fine countries were represented at this gathering, but it was certainly an impressive sight, making me feel, for maybe the first time since my youth, proud of my native city.

However, as the mayor (White-British, of course; developments hadn't yet come *that* far in Bradford) continued with his speech — including much sound-bite talk about "integration" and "social harmony" and "working together to achieve [X and Y]" — I spotted other people in the crowds, ones decidedly less well-disposed to such warm words.

Most wore sunglasses, and some looked apprehensively restless. I was hardly surprised by that; after all, this was what all their recent activities had been leading up to, ones that I alone seemed to have stumbled upon. Nevertheless, none of the creatures moved, persuading me to think that whatever subterfuge they planned — spiking all the food and drink with drugs — had already been performed. They'd possibly added these substances prior to delivery, having violated storage places reserved for it all. At such a public event, this incoming produce had surely been regulated, and so they'd have worked surreptitiously, maybe breaking in while drawing on every resource provided by their flexible limbs and furtive, all-round vision.

Everything was, as the distinguished speaker started bringing his talk to a close, about to kick off.

Turning back to face Sara Edgeley, packing as much information into as few words as possible, I told her all I knew about the felachnids.

Once I'd finished, about a minute later, she stared at me as if I was more freakish than even the creatures I'd just described. Although I'd prepared the ground to some degree during my interview, I'd changed, in just a few days, from an amused sceptic to a rabid believer. And what did that imply about my mental health, about what those evil entities had done to my mind?

These were surely questions the woman asked herself, her eyes shining as strikingly as they always had. Her body, too, looked sharp and firm, smartly attired in another tight dress. And yet she *did nothing*, simply stood staring my way, until I sensed her gaze wither, as if her face had changed somehow, appearing less genuine than it had recently, when she and I had ended up in bed together, enjoying frantic, anatomically challenging tumbles, which had left me stretched and strained.

"*Well*? Will you *help* me?" I asked, no longer sure if I was even sane.

"But, Lee, I...I..." she replied, and I immediately sensed that her mind was elsewhere, maybe on the activities just behind her, which now appeared to be drawing to a close. At that moment, her face changed, as if she'd drawn confidence from what was happening nearby, and then she looked at me once more with that intense blue gaze. And smiled. "Just in time," she said at last.

Her inactivity dismaying me almost as much as her obvious amusement now troubled me, I twisted away from Sara, addressing the group of relatively eminent people under the canopy. That was when the mayor announced his concluding words, "I now declare this great event open and sincerely hope you all have a memorable time."

Few of them looked quite right, either, just as Sara didn't now. Here were members of local power-groups — councils, the legal system, and many other essential administrative institutions in a community — but none seemed as pleasurably humble as they should in such an important situation. Indeed, as in the journalist at the moment, there was a tangible species of glee perceptible among them, so much so that it had infected their faces to an extraordinary degree.

No, not their faces.

Their *eyes*.

That was when, as the mass of people sprawling right across the park — surely close to 100,000 already — began retreating to join in the fun, I turned back to face Sara... and saw what she'd done to her head.

She was peeling it back, her face twisted awkwardly over one shoulder. Her right arm, the one with which she carried out this tricky manoeuvre, was bent at a weird angle, moving so far against the natural range of a standard elbow that, for one foolish moment, I fancied it might shatter the bone. But then I saw what she was really doing, and how easily she managed to do so: removing contact lenses. *Blue* contact lenses.

Seconds later, she was exposed for the fraud she was — her yellow eyes glaring like sickly fire — and, in a sudden flash of painful insight, I realised so many things simultaneously: the way she'd comfortably held her alcohol that night, while I'd been nearly drunk after only a few glasses; the reason she'd been so eager to get that newspaper article printed so quickly, presumably an under-the-radar warning to all her city-based colleagues that someone was on to them; the way I'd been tracked for days by people wearing shades, the first in the pub with John Marsh, a spy who might even have been in touch with Sara, prompting her message to me the same day; and then the athletic sex we'd enjoyed, the room left pitch-dark to prevent me from perceiving the true nature of my amour — the flexing limbs, that swivelling skull, and those devilish eyes: the ones now staring fiercely my way.

I'd underestimated the felachnids; their disruptive influence in pitiable Bradford extended way beyond mere street-corner scrotes and house-burglars wrestling around for scraps of cash. They'd also infiltrated many high places in the community, including recently elected dignitaries with unimpeachable reputations. For one naïve moment, I figured this was why those who'd joined society, deploying disguises in the form of coloured contact lenses, had been unable to make their bank accounts free for the sort of money-raising activities the lesser creatures must resort to.

But then I thought better of that conclusion. The simple fact was that those shade-wearing freaks had been sent into the community to cause menace, cross-wiring many people, the affluent against the poor, the healthy against the sick, Brits against Poles, and surely many other amusingly sadistic combinations. It was all a sick game to them, but actually more than that: it was tradition, the calling-card of their species. Indeed, their more advanced colleagues — those now in high positions — might have easily financed the venture from salaries drawn from their roles, but where was the fun in that? It didn't maximise corruption, didn't warm up the community for the main event. Besides, those invading houses and taking what they needed were perhaps learning the subversive skills their seniors already possessed, allowing them one day to acquire rival power and status.

I needn't have turned back to the group behind me to realise many of them had also removed their masks, that final semblance of humanity, becoming those yellow-eyed cat-spider creatures I'd sought for days. And why shouldn't they now expose their true nature? Their task was complete, after all.

They were a malignant species, genetically programmed to cause unrest. They were the enemies of everything this city had ever tried to achieve: ethnic integration, cultural diversity, multiracial tolerance. They leeched upon people, because that was how evolution worked, the biological profile of any life-form developing in co-existence with proximate others. The felachnids had possibly landed on earth, many hundreds of years ago; their immediate targets had been residents of a tiny village in North

Yorkshire, and it had taken a long time for the entities to become so organised, to spread their poison further, to target the biggest venue of all: migration down the valleys to Bradford, where civil coexistence was gunpowder simply in need of a spark.

I now looked across the grand park in which this celebratory event was being staged. Everywhere, people were clustered around eateries, ready to dine. A BBC camera-crew was stationed beside its logo-marked van parked near the entrance. Whatever followed, stage-managed by the insidious people behind me with their newly disposable careers, would be broadcasted right across the country, maybe even the world. I no longer wondered why Sara Edgeley wasn't making notes for the Telegraph and Argus; there was no need for such minor coverage when she and her accomplices had the whole planet to target.

How deep did this institutional infection lie? I recalled thinking about how little crime was reported in the local newspaper — did that suggest its editor was involved, too? I looked around, spotting various senior police officers, one even wearing shades. Christ, were they *all* in on this — or at least, enough people in positions of authority to make it happen?

Meanwhile, countless others ahead of me had started to consume the various delights on offer, always the chief attraction at the mela. Somewhere a band began playing, its tune incongruously joyous and yet soon to shift to a minor key. Above, clouds gathered, bellies heavy with potential rain. I suddenly didn't know what to do.

In the event, I whirled around, facing my new adversaries. They all stood there, yellow eyes exposed to onlookers, as if they didn't care now who knew their true nature. Every one of them had played a role in bringing about this corruption: uniformed sergeants overlooking the exploitation of vulnerable groups; journalists ensuring crime reports about the felachnids' activities appeared infrequently in local media; councillors coordinating activities between different community groups. It had been a carefully arranged plan, involving few lapses in role expectations, but now that the objective had been achieved, its orchestrators, with mad gazes and rippling limbs, look ready to party.

And what could *I* do about this? I let my gaze roam around the area, again taking in the many police officers patrolling at various distances. I couldn't be certain that all were affiliated to the nefarious plot, but enough might be for me to choose the wrong one to engage with. It surely wasn't worth the risk.

Closer by, however, I noticed the vacant microphone, which remained active, its PA equipment still thrumming in the wake of the mayor's speech. Without any further thought, I made a quick dash for this, grabbing the mike at once and beginning to deliver my impromptu message to the turned-away masses.

"*Listen, everyone, you mustn't eat anyth—*" I began, but before I could say any more, the amplified sound went dead, leaving only my feeble voice crying out to the crowd across more than five hundred yards. Nobody could hear me; what with the constant buzz of chatter all around the place, I could hardly hear myself.

I turned immediately, noticing a guy standing near the system's chunky speakers, a fat jack-plug in one hand which he'd clearly just removed from a giant amplifier. He'd disconnected the sound network just as soon as I'd begun speaking. I wasn't at all surprised to see that this man had bright yellow eyes and that his sound technician's outfit was twisted out of shape by sickeningly misaligned limbs. He also smiled a maniac's smile.

That expression angered me, but perhaps only because of how

useless it made me feel. Indeed, moments later, I rushed for this man, trying to grab that jack-plug and wire from his twisting-turning hand. But before I even reached him, several others were upon me, those *things* rushing forwards to prevent any further disruption to their glorious event.

I struggled and protested, but it was no good: the men who now had hold of me were not much bigger than I, but in greater numbers. I was easily pulled away before I could cause any more disruption. They eventually thrust me to the ground several yards from the PA system, close to all those local luminaries again, who had no business with me, simply desiring to cause damage to a much larger target: my native city, with which I'd always had such a love-hate relationship.

Just at that moment, I'd never felt less optimistic in my life, not even when I'd heard about Glenn's death and had raged at the world for weeks afterwards. I'd become empty inside, feeling utterly hopeless. All my studies on social relations seemed to drift away in a breeze. I got up, dusting myself off, but then, looking slowly at each of my sinister, hissing, triumphant observers in turn, I started speaking, drawing with intuitive haste upon a lifetime of research.

"You're all little more than a *scourge*. The fact that, to be true to yourselves, you have to see others unhappy is nothing more than *envy*. Your nature isn't written in the stars. In complex behaviours, like you and my species share, I believe nothing can be proved to be so. You *learned* to be this way — after being shut out and treated as scapegoats, so many years ago, when humans knew no better.

"And have things changed since? I can't say that they have. But you know what? Whatever misfortunes you all suffered during your early existence, after first arriving on this planet, you've no excuses now. You're little more than hooligans, than folk who smash up phone-boxes because they're excluded from a world they secretly wish to be part of, if only they could join in and get by. All this means only one thing: *nobody who is happy behaves badly.* I feel that deeply in my heart. So let me share the conclusion of my latest research."

Feeling acerbic, my eyes finally settled on those of Sara Edgeley, who, without her blue contact lenses, looked as frightening as the rest of her coterie. I recalled the acrobatic acts we'd enjoyed together a few nights earlier; the thought of being intimate with one of *them* was less alarming than what she presently did with her arms and legs: twisted them backwards until she resembled an insect rendered only tenuously in human form. All the others were performing similar acts, their heads also bent back, until they appeared to be glaring at me with those savage yellow eyes from impossible anatomical angles. I didn't see any examples of that tell-tale logo on their clothing, but wouldn't have been surprised if I had.

I realised they were celebrating, their bodies cavorting with barely contained ecstasy. But this was no plastic sensation, the kind elicited by tawdry toxic substances. This was the *real deal*, the summation of much strategic preparation. They might have a decidedly limited goal in mind — the destabilisation of race relations in one of the UK's most delicately balanced cultural locations — but they'd nonetheless achieved it with considerable gusto.

From behind, I heard the first of surely many people register the impact of violent drugs in their systems: someone screamed with rage, and then another with terror. But that didn't stop me drawing my project synopsis to a close.

"My conclusion is that *misery masquerades as disruptive glee*, and that however many other people are fooled by that kind of behaviour, *it always secretly remains misery*. And I truly think that such corruption lies so deep in your souls that you'll never escape this truth. *Never.*"

For one brief moment, barely detectable at all, I saw a few of the things hesitate, yellow eyes flickering, as if their successful period had just been compromised. But then they went back to enjoying the whole spectacle, as more screams and shouts and other sounds of violence being enacted way behind me started filling the area with horror.

I was unable to stay, could do nothing more to help. There was only one of me, and thousands of them. Isn't *that* often the tragic truth of our species? And so I walked away, satisfied that I'd said what I'd wanted to say, the thing I'd learnt recently or had possibly had reinforced in my modest pool of knowledge. I sensed the spirit of Glenn, my late brother, settle down in my head, and then continued moving, out from the park all its terrifying events, with TV cameras waiting to inform the world, along with so many innocent people who'd just wanted to get along today, as on every day.

And isn't that *all* of us, really?

I didn't watch the news later that day; it sometimes makes me forget who we truly are.

THE BUREAU OF THEM

Cate Gardner

You're not the first to talk to your dead here, the vagrant said. The living always chase after their dead until they come upon their own.

Formed from shadow and dust, ghosts inhabit the abandoned office building, angry at the world that denies them. When Katy sees her deceased boyfriend in the window of the derelict building, she finds a way in, hoping to be reunited. Instead, the dead ignore, the dead do not see and only the monster that is Yarker Ryland has need of her there.

WITHIN THE WIND,

BENEATH THE SNOW

Ray Cluley

Gjerta knew there were darkteeth in the woods. They lived amongst the trees and in the shadows between them.
And they were always there.
Hidden. Quietly waiting.

Out of sight, but always in her mind...

SNOWBOOKS HORROR NOVELLAS

THE GREENS

Andrew Hook

Two green—skinned children are discovered who claim to have come from within the earth. The local legend states that the boy died, and the girl married but had no children. Is the legend true?

OCD sufferers often perpetuate their rituals believing that if they fail to do so their families will suffer. But what if they are correct — that their rituals are necessary to maintain life's balance?

And what if it was discovered that many OCD sufferers are descendants of the green children...

www.snowbooks.com